My Genius Me

My Genius Me

MALACHI AND MALIKA'S EXTRAORDINARY QUEST: UNLOCKING THE SECRETS OF SUCCESS

Melenie Hibbert

MGM Publishing

This book is dedicated to my inner child.
If I knew these things when I was young,
life would be very different today...

I am grateful to be able to bring this
knowledge to the younger generation
so they can go forth and be
their true MAGNIFICENT self.

Contents

Foreword by Sophia Bailey-Larsen

When it comes to genius fuelled by a burning desire, Melenie Hibbert is one of the first names that comes to mind. Melenie has taken the problems that many families face, and created a solution by introducing the principles for success used by the most brilliant people in the world and teaching them to children.

I have had the pleasure of talking to Melenie about her passion for transforming the lives of young people for several years so it's an absolute joy to be introducing her book on the topic. As a mother of three myself, I can envision the impact this book could make to families who take the time to read it together.

My Genius Me, is a unique combination of fiction and non-fiction based on the book 'Think and Grow Rich' by Napoleon Hill. Having taught Hill's work for over a decade, I know the impact it has made to my mentees in every area of their lives from health and relationships, to business and of course riches.

You are no different, by changing your thinking you can change your life.

Melenie's passion is serving young people that are on the cusp of being influenced by society. This is the point where many become distracted from their goals and can enter a downward spiral. By learning about the power of their mind, children can be empowered to make informed decisions. I'm excited by her vision to transform an entire generation beginning with this quest to unlock the secrets of success.

Each chapter of My Genius Me, delves into one success principle in a way that shows an understanding of the huge pressure on our children while they explore their dreams of the future. The main characters share how they feel about the growing expectations of them in today's world and the book arms them with exercises to overcome the challenges and keep moving towards your dreams.

I encourage teachers and parents to work through these activities with your children. Let's envision a world with more Malachi's, Malika's and even Melenie's who discover their genius within.

I wish you all the best on your Quest.

Sophia Bailey-Larsen Leading Certified Instructor for the Napoleon Hill Foundation

Creator of The Science of Thinking Rich™ and The Vision Creation Experience™

Foreword by MMAM

I have known Melenie for ten years. We were first introduced via social media by a mutual associate.

It wasn't too long after that we met in person at Croydon Library to passionately discuss the business of educating our young generation and their families by organising events within the local community and schools.

There is a constant flow of testimonial growth, emotional growth, academic growth, family growth; showing Melenie is evidently purposed to create therapeutic experiences accompanied with bespoke resources for successful outcomes.

Over the many years of working closely with Melenie she remains committed to empowering individuals to activate the genius within them.

My Genius Me demonstrates how a healthy mind determines excellent performance.

Your emotions and thoughts can be very difficult to speak about, regulate or admit. Very often you may keep them secretly in your head because you are afraid that others may not understand.

Your mind is your hard drive that stores your thoughts; about yourself and the world around you. It is your choice what you save and what you delete.

What you believe about yourself determines your success or failure.

You are about to explore a mindful journey that will transform your mindset. You will think different. You will feel different. You will do different.

This is a safe journey, that will challenge and confront old mindset to become the new you.

This book has been personally created for you to be the Marvellous Mind.

Remember you are fearfully and wonderfully made.

If you dream it. If you believe it. You can do it.

Marcia Anderson McKenzie

Author's Introduction

My inspiration for this book first came about when I was just beginning my own self-improvement journey in the first few years of my teaching career.

As a parent with a young child, faced with the challenges in school, teaching, managing my students' needs, striving to be the best teacher I could be, I needed to find a better way to cope with all that I had going on and turned to self-improvement to help me.

As I was going through this process, whilst standing in front of my class, teaching, the thought struck me 'If only I knew this stuff when I was their age, surely my life would have turned out different?' I would have had the faith, belief, desire and persistence to go for my dreams and be confident in myself to actually achieve it! It was at this point that the seed was sown to teach these principles to children, so that they can flourish throughout their lives, in education and beyond. Transforming a generation to believe that they can Be, Do, Have anything they desire.

The principles I'm referring to, comes from the book Think and Grow Rich by Napoleon Hill. This book was first published in 1937 and is still a best seller today. Why? The principles are the truth and will always be the truth and therefore always will be relevant in all times.

In the author's introduction of Think and Grow Rich, Napoleon Hill states:

'This book contains the secret, after having been put to a practical test by thousands of people, in almost every walk of life. It was Mr.

Carnegie's idea that the magic formula, which gave him a stupendous fortune, ought to be placed within reach of people who do not have time to investigate how men make money, and it was his hope that I might test and demonstrate the soundness of the formula through the experience of men and women in every calling. He believed the formula should be taught in all public schools and colleges, and expressed the opinion that if it were properly taught it would so revolutionise the entire educational system that the time spent in school could be reduced to less than half.

His experience with Charles M. Schwab, and other young men of Mr. Schwab's type, convinced Mr. Carnegie that much of that which is taught in the schools is of no value whatsoever in connection with the business of earning a living or accumulating riches. He had arrived at this decision, because he had taken into his business one young man after another, many of them with but little schooling, and by coaching them in the use of this formula, developed in them rare leadership. Moreover, his coaching made fortunes for every one of them who followed his instructions.'

This is something I truly believe, therefore set about to get it in the hands of parents to begin to teach these principles to their children and develop in them the ability to create and achieve anything they desire.

Over 100 years ago Henry Ford said, "Whether you think you can or think you can't, you're right!" He was pointing to the way our beliefs colour our perceptions of reality by filtering the millions of possible outcomes to the ones that match our beliefs.

If our beliefs are aligned to what we desire and we are certain both about what we want and our ability to attain it, we view every person, circumstances and opportunities as an ally, a friend, someone or something that can help us achieve our goals and aspirations. However, if we are guided by an internal script that says it's not possible, I'm not worthy, I'm not capable; we lock ourselves into a mindset that screams **LACK** and a self-fulfilling prophecy of never achieving the life we desire which then reinforces our limiting self-beliefs.

Beliefs are simply thoughts that have been thought over and over again!

Like a well-worn path that goes from point A to point B, relentlessly!

Our beliefs are formed when we are young and our brain is soaking up all the information that informs our world at a young age. There is a huge amount of research that shows how our beliefs, formed in childhood, impacts the rest of our adult lives. This gives us even more reason to ensure that we empower our children's mind-sets to create beliefs that allows them to believe in what they want and their ability to achieve it.

My Genius Me – Malachi and Malika's Extraordinary Quest: Unlocking the Secrets of Success

Principles for Life!

Melenie Hibbert

1

～

The Mysterious Invitation

Malachi and Malika sat at the kitchen table, engrossed in their favourite science book. They marvelled at the pictures of faraway galaxies and dreamed of exploring the universe. Both of them had big dreams, and they knew that the secrets to achieving them were hidden within the pages of books.

All of a sudden, the doorbell rang without warning, interrupting their daydreaming. Malachi's dad, Mr. Johnson, answered the door and returned with an intriguing envelope in his hand. It had an elegant golden seal and was addressed to 'Malachi and Malika, Seekers of Knowledge.'

Curiosity sparked in their eyes as they eagerly tore open the envelope. Inside, they found a beautifully handwritten letter, inviting them on a mysterious adventure. It read:

Dear Malachi and Malika,

You have shown great passion for learning and an insatiable thirst for knowledge. I invite you to embark on a once-in-a-lifetime journey to unlock the secrets of greatness.

Meet me at the Hidden Library, nestled deep within the enchanted forest, on the morning of the next full moon. Follow the twinkling stars as your guide. Prepare to discover ancient wisdom and ignite the power within you.

Yours sincerely,
The Guardian of Knowledge

Malachi and Malika's eyes widened with excitement. They looked at each other, their hearts pounding with anticipation. This was the opportunity they had been waiting for, a chance to unravel the mysteries of success and achieve their dreams.

As the full moon cast its enchanting glow upon the forest, Malachi and Malika tiptoed out of their homes and followed the trail of twinkling stars. The air was crisp, and the scent of adventure filled their lungs.

They ventured deeper into the forest, their excitement growing with each step. As they walked, they noticed the trees whispering ancient secrets, as if guiding them toward their destination. Finally, they arrived at a clearing, where a magnificent library stood, bathed in moonlight.

The library's doors creaked open, inviting them inside. The moment they crossed the threshold, a warm glow wrapped around them, and they felt an invisible force drawing them closer to a figure shrouded in shadows.

The figure revealed itself as the Guardian of Knowledge, a wise and kind mentor. With a gentle smile, the guardian welcomed Malachi and Malika, explaining that they were chosen for their hunger for knowledge and their desire to make a difference in the world.

"Young seekers," the guardian spoke, "Within this library lies a hidden treasure—a book called 'Think and Grow Rich.' It holds the keys to unlocking your true potential and achieving greatness. But be warned, this journey will require courage, dedication, and an unwavering belief in yourself."

Malachi and Malika exchanged determined glances, ready to embark on this extraordinary quest. They knew that this was the beginning of an adventure that would change their lives forever.

With the mysterious invitation as their guide and the guardian as their mentor, Malachi and Malika eagerly stepped deeper into the library. The pages of 'Think and Grow Rich' beckoned, promising them a world of untapped possibilities.

Little did they know that their lives were about to be transformed, as they embarked on a journey filled with challenges, lessons, and the discovery of their true potential.

2

〰

Meeting the Wise Mentor

Malachi and Malika stood in awe as the doors of the library closed behind them. The room was filled with ancient books, their spines lined with gold and silver, emanating a sense of wisdom and magic. Soft candlelight danced across the shelves, casting a warm glow on the rows of knowledge.

From amidst the shelves, a figure emerged, stepping into the light. It was the Guardian of Knowledge, their mysterious mentor. With a calm yet commanding presence, he greeted them warmly.

"Welcome, Malachi and Malika," the guardian said with a wise smile. "I have been waiting for your arrival. The universe has brought you here to embark on a profound journey of self-discovery and growth."

Malachi and Malika exchanged glances, their hearts pounding with excitement. They could sense that this mentor held the keys to unlocking their hidden potential.

The guardian continued, "As I said previously, within this library, you will find the secrets of 'Think and Grow Rich,' a book that has guided countless individuals to success. Its wisdom transcends time and empowers those who embrace its principles."

Curiosity twinkled in Malachi's eyes as he asked, "But what is the true purpose of this journey? What do we hope to achieve?"

The guardian paused for a moment, contemplating his question. With a gentle smile, he responded, "The purpose, my young friends, is to unleash the infinite power that lies within each of you. 'Think and Grow Rich' is not just about material wealth; it is about realising your dreams, achieving your goals, and becoming the best version of yourselves."

Malachi and Malika nodded, their determination growing stronger. They were ready to embrace this transformative journey and discover their true potential.

The guardian led them to a cosy reading area, adorned with plush chairs and a crackling fireplace. As they settled in, the guardian reached for a weathered copy of 'Think and Grow Rich' and placed it in their hands.

"This book," the guardian explained, "is a roadmap to success. It contains principles that, when applied diligently, can lead you to greatness. But remember, the true power lies within you. This book is merely a guide, and it is up to you to take the lessons and apply them to your lives."

Malachi and Malika nodded, their eyes fixated on the book's worn pages. They understood the weight of the knowledge that lay before them.

The guardian continued, "In the chapters that lie within this book, you will explore the principles of desire, faith, specialised knowledge, imagination, decision-making, persistence, the power of a mastermind, the subconscious mind, the power of the brain, the sixth sense and outwitting the ghost of fear. Each principle holds its own magic, guiding you closer to your dreams."

Excitement bubbled within Malachi and Malika as they realised the immense possibilities that awaited them. They were ready to dive into the depths of this ancient wisdom, to absorb the teachings and integrate them into their lives.

"Remember," the guardian emphasised, "this journey requires dedication, discipline, and an unwavering belief in yourselves. Stay committed to your goals, and let the principles of 'Think and Grow Rich' guide you towards the stars."

Malachi and Malika nodded solemnly, their determination shining in their eyes.

"To begin, let's look at the power of our thoughts."

"The power of our thoughts?" Malachi asked, puzzled.

"Yes, Malachi," the guardian replied. "Our thoughts have the power to create our reality. If we think positively, we attract positive things into our lives, including wealth."

Malachi and Malika were fascinated. They wanted to know more.

"Thoughts are things," the guardian said.

"Thoughts are things?" Malika repeated, trying to make sense of it.

"Yes, Malika. Our thoughts are like seeds that we plant in our minds. If we plant positive thoughts, we will reap positive results. But if we plant negative thoughts, we will reap negative results," the guardian explained.

Malika nodded, understanding the analogy.

"Our thoughts have the power to shape our reality. Everything we see around us, from buildings to cars to airplanes, started as a thought in someone's mind. Every great invention, every successful business, every book, every piece of art began with a thought."

Malachi and Malika were amazed. They had never thought of it that way before.

"Your thoughts are powerful," the guardian continued. "They have the power to create your reality. If you think positively, you will attract positive things into your life. But if you think negatively, you will attract negative things."

Malachi thought about it for a moment. "So, if I think positively about getting good grades, I will get good grades?"

"Exactly!" the guardian said. "Your thoughts have the power to influence your actions and decisions, which in turn affect your outcomes. If you believe that you can do well in school and you work hard, you will get good grades."

Malachi was excited. He realised that he had the power to shape his own destiny!

"But what about bad things?" Malika asked. "If I think positively, will bad things never happen to me?"

"Bad things can happen to anyone, Malika," the guardian said. "But if you have a positive mindset, you will be better equipped to deal with challenges and bounce back from setbacks. You will also attract positive people and opportunities into your life that can help you overcome obstacles."

Malika nodded, understanding the concept. "So, if I want to be successful, I need to think positively?"

"Exactly," the guardian said. "Your thoughts have the power to shape your reality. If you want to be successful, you need to think like a successful person. You need to believe in yourself and your abilities, and you need to take action to make your dreams a reality."

Malachi and Malika were inspired. They couldn't wait to learn more about the other principles of 'Think and Grow Rich' and put them into practice in their own life. They realised that the power of their thoughts was greater than they had ever imagined, and they were determined to use it to achieve their goals.

The guardian concluded, "Your journey begins now, young seekers of knowledge. May you find the wisdom and strength you seek within the pages of this book. Embrace the lessons, apply them to your lives, and watch as your dreams come to fruition."

With those parting words, Malachi and Malika delved into the world of 'Think and Grow Rich,' ready to unlock the secrets of success and shape their destinies.

Activity: Who Am I?

Begin your quest by discovery where you currently perceive yourself to be as your starting point.

Take the time and really be as honest as possible when answering these questions.

There is no judgement, this is a journey of self-reflection and empowerment!

Who Am I?

• How would you describe yourself?

• How would your family describe you?

• How would your friends describe you?

• How would your teachers describe you?

• How would you describe the person you want to be?

Your Reflections

3

∾

The Magic of Dream Seeds: Igniting Your Passion

Malachi and Malika sat cross-legged on the soft carpeted floor of the Hidden Library, their eyes fixed on the pages of 'Think and Grow Rich.' Excitement pulsed through their veins as they delved into the first principle: Desire.

The words on the pages seemed to come alive, whispering ancient secrets of achievement and success. Malachi and Malika learned that desire was the starting point for all great achievements, the spark that ignited the flame of ambition within.

Malika closed her eyes and envisioned herself as a renowned scientist, exploring the vast wonders of the universe. She felt a deep yearning within her, a burning desire to uncover the mysteries of the cosmos and make ground-breaking discoveries. Her heart raced with excitement.

Malachi, too, felt the fire of desire within him. He imagined himself as an inventor, creating innovative technologies to propel humanity forward. He wanted to leave a lasting impact on the world and make a difference in people's lives. The intensity of his desire surged through him like a tidal wave of motivation.

The guardian, observing their contemplation, smiled knowingly. "Desire is the fuel that drives us to take action," he explained. "It is the unwavering belief in our dreams and the determination to bring them to fruition. Without desire, dreams remain dormant, but with it, they can become a reality."

Malachi raised his hand, eager to understand more. "But how do we cultivate and strengthen our desire?" he asked.

The guardian nodded, appreciating the young boy's thirst for knowledge. "Desire is nurtured through clarity and focus," he answered. "Take the time to identify your true passions and align them with your goals. Visualise your dreams with vivid detail, imagining the joy and fulfilment they would bring."

Malika spoke up, her voice filled with determination. "I desire to be a scientist exploring the universe. I want to understand the mysteries of space and contribute to scientific knowledge."

The guardian nodded approvingly. "That is a powerful desire, Malika. Now, let that desire guide your actions. Immerse yourself in scientific studies, read books, visit observatories, and engage with like-minded individuals. Let your desire propel you forward, even in the face of challenges."

Malachi added, "I desire to be an inventor, creating technologies that change the world. I want to make life better for people and leave a lasting legacy."

The guardian smiled, impressed by Malachi's clarity of purpose. "Your desire is admirable, Malachi. Let it fuel your creativity and drive you to learn and experiment. Embrace failure as a stepping stone towards success, for it is through persistence that desire transforms into reality."

As Malachi and Malika absorbed the wisdom, a newfound determination settled within them. They understood that desire was not merely a wishful thought; it was a powerful force that could guide their actions and shape their destinies.

The guardian concluded, "Remember, my young seekers, desire is the first step towards greatness. Cultivate it, nurture it, and let it guide you on your journey. The universe responds to those who truly desire and are willing to work diligently towards their dreams."

Malachi and Malika closed their eyes, taking a moment to visualise their desires and feel the burning passion within them. They knew that this was just the beginning, and with their desires as their compass, they were ready to set sail on a grand adventure.

~~~~~~

As Malachi and Malika continued their journey alongside their wise mentor, they found themselves facing a crucial point. It was time to delve into the first principle: Desire. The mentor knew that true success could only be achieved when fuelled by a burning passion and an unwavering commitment to one's dreams.

To ignite the flame of desire within Malachi and Malika, their mentor devised a series of interactive activities and captivating storytelling sessions. He wanted them to uncover their deepest desires and understand the power they held within.

The first activity involved creating a vision board. Malachi and Malika gathered magazines, scissors, glue, and large sheets of paper. They spent hours flipping through the pages, carefully cutting out images and words that resonated with their dreams of exploring the universe as scientists and inventors. They glued these fragments onto their vision boards, creating colourful collages that visually represented their aspirations.

As they admired their vision boards, the mentor shared stories of famous scientists who had pursued their passions with unwavering determination. He recounted the tales of Garret Morgan, Lewis Howard Latimer, Albert Einstein, Dr Mae Jemison, Dr. Aprille Ericsson-Jackson, Patricia Bath and Dr. Shirley Ann Jackson highlighting their relentless pursuit of knowledge and their contributions to the field of science and invention. Through these stories, Malachi and Malika realised that their dreams were not just fantasies but were within their reach with dedication and perseverance.

Next, their mentor encouraged them to engage in reflective journaling. Each day, Malachi and Malika would write about their dreams, describing in vivid detail what it would be like to explore distant galaxies, create new inventions, discover new planets, and unlock the secrets of the universe. They let their imagination run wild, immersing themselves in a world where possibilities were endless.

During their mentorship sessions, Malachi and Malika also engaged in open and honest discussions about their desires. They shared their fears, their doubts, and their wildest dreams. The mentor listened attentively, offering guidance and support, reminding them that the road to success might be challenging, but the fire within them would keep them going.

Through these activities, Malachi and Malika discovered that their desires were more than fleeting interests. They were passions that burned deep within their souls, driving them to pursue their dreams with unwavering dedication.

As their understanding of desire grew, so did their commitment. They realised that success wasn't just about achieving external goals; it was about the journey of growth, learning, and self-discovery along the way. They embraced the idea that their desires were unique to them, and their journey would reflect their own dreams and aspirations.

With the fire of desire burning brightly within them, Malachi and Malika embarked on the next phase of their journey with renewed energy and determination. They knew that challenges would arise, but their unwavering commitment to their dreams would carry them through.

And so, with hearts ablaze with passion and determination, Malachi and Malika continued their journey, ready to face whatever challenges lay ahead, fuelled by the power of desire.

Activity: Discovering Your Desires

Objective: To help you explore your passions, interests, and desires in order to gain clarity about your goals and aspirations.

Materials needed:

• Paper, pens or pencils, art supplies (optional).

Instructions:

Begin by creating a relaxed and comfortable environment for the activity. Find a quiet space where you can reflect and express yourself freely.

Take a few deep breaths and relax your body and mind.

On a piece of paper, write or draw about things that make you happy, excited, or curious.

Create a list, make a mind map, or draw pictures of your interests and passions.
There are no right or wrong answers, and you can include anything that resonates with you.

Think about your favourite activities, subjects in school, hobbies, and things you enjoy doing in your free time.

Consider your dreams and aspirations for the future.

After you have created your list or artwork, reflect on each item and think about why it brings you joy or curiosity.

• What do you love about this activity or subject?
• How does it make you feel when you engage in it?

- What do you find fascinating or interesting about it?
- How would you like to explore this interest further?
- What steps do you think you can take to learn more about it or pursue it?
- Can you envision yourself doing this as a career or a lifelong passion?

Choose one or two desires or interests that resonate with you the most.

These choices don't have to be set in stone but are simply starting points for your journey of self-discovery.

It's important to pursue your passions and setting goals based on your desires.
Your desires can guide you towards a fulfilling and meaningful life.

Continue exploring your desires and passions, it's okay to change your goals and aspirations as you grow and learn.

Remember, the purpose of this activity is to help you tap into your desires and gain clarity about your interests and explore your unique passions.

Your Reflections

4

~

Believe and Achieve: Deep Within You

Malachi and Malika sat in anticipation as they turned the pages of 'Think and Grow Rich' to uncover the second principle: Faith. They knew that without faith, their dreams would remain distant and un-attainable.

The guardian smiled warmly, sensing their eagerness to learn. "Faith," he began, "is the unwavering belief in yourself, your abilities, and the realisation that anything is possible. It is the fuel that keeps your dreams alive even in the face of adversity. Faith is also more than just a belief in oneself. It is a deep, unshakable trust in something greater than oneself, whether it be a higher power or simply the power of the universe."

Malachi thought about what this meant and realised that he had always believed in something greater than himself. He also believed in the power of hard work, dedication, and determination to help him achieve his goals.

Malachi furrowed his brow, pondering the concept. "But how do we develop such strong faith?" he asked.

The guardian nodded understandingly. "Faith is built upon a foundation of self-belief and positive thinking," he explained. "It starts by recognising your strengths and acknowledging your potential. Believe in your own abilities and trust that you have what it takes to achieve your dreams. Your faith will be developed and strengthened over time. It isn't something that just happens overnight, but rather a gradual process of building trust and confidence in oneself and one's abilities."

Malika chimed in, her eyes shining with determination. "So, even when things get tough, we must continue to have faith in ourselves and our dreams?"

The guardian nodded, his voice filled with reassurance. "Indeed, Malika. Challenges will inevitably come your way, but with unwavering faith, you will find the strength and resilience to overcome them. Trust that every setback is an opportunity for growth and learning. Faith is a crucial component of success. Without it, one could easily become discouraged and give up when faced with setbacks or obstacles. But with faith, one could keep pushing forward and trust that everything would work out in the end."

Malachi's face lit up with understanding. "So, even if others doubt us or if we face setbacks, we must hold onto our faith and keep moving forward?"

The guardian smiled proudly. "Exactly, Malachi. Your faith will become a shield against negativity and doubt. Surround yourself with positive influences, seek support from those who believe in you, and remember that the power to manifest your dreams lies within your unwavering faith."

Malika thought about the times she had faced setbacks or failures. There were times when she felt like giving up, but she had always found the strength to keep going. She realised that this was because she had faith that she could achieve her goals, no matter what.

The children absorbed the wisdom, realising that faith was not just a blind hope but a force that could shape their reality. They closed their eyes, envisioning their dreams with unwavering faith, feeling the emotions as if they had already achieved them.

The guardian encouraged them, "Embrace your dreams with every fibre of your being. See them as already accomplished, and let that belief guide your actions. Trust that the universe is conspiring in your favour."

Malika spoke with conviction, her voice filled with newfound faith. "I have faith that I will become a renowned scientist exploring the universe. I trust in my abilities, and I am ready to face any challenges that come my way."

Malachi echoed her sentiment. "I have faith in my inventions and my potential to make a positive impact. I believe in my ability to create change and improve lives."

The guardian smiled, his eyes sparkling with pride. "Your faith is strong, my young seekers. Hold onto it fiercely, for it will be your guiding light on this journey of success."

Malachi and Malika opened their eyes, their hearts filled with a renewed sense of purpose. They understood that faith was not just a belief, but an active force that propelled them forward. With each step they took, they would do so with unwavering faith in their dreams.

The guardian concluded, "Remember, my young friends, faith is the bridge that connects your desires to their realisation. Embrace it, nurture it, and watch as it shapes your destiny."

~~~~~~~~~~~~~~~~~~~~~~~~~~~~~~~~~

Malachi and Malika's journey of scientific exploration had led them to discover the incredible power of unwavering faith. As they faced a series of challenges and uncertainties, they learned to trust in themselves and their dreams.

One sunny morning, as they set out on a daring experiment, doubts started to creep into their minds. The task seemed daunting, and the fear of failure loomed over them like a dark cloud. But deep within, they knew that their dreams were worth pursuing, and they had to summon their unwavering faith to overcome their doubts.

Their mentor sensed their unease and gathered them for a heart-to-heart discussion. "Faith is like a guiding light in the darkest of times," he said. "It is the unwavering belief in yourself, your abilities, and the ultimate outcome of your dreams. It is the fuel that propels you forward, even when the path seems uncertain."

He reminded them that having faith also meant being patient and trusting in the timing of things. Sometimes, things might not happen as quickly as one would like, but that didn't mean they weren't happening at all. It was important to trust in the process and have faith that everything would work out in the end.

Their mentor shared stories of great scientists who had faced numerous obstacles and setbacks but had triumphed in the end because of their unwavering faith. Malachi and Malika listened intently, drawing inspiration from these tales of resilience and determination.

To deepen their understanding of faith, the mentor led them through a series of challenging exercises. They were asked to confront their doubts and fears head-on, acknowledging their existence but refusing to let them control their actions.

They took part in visualisation exercises, closing their eyes and picturing themselves succeeding in their endeavours. They imagined the feeling of accomplishment, the joy of discovery, and the impact they would have on the world.

Throughout these exercises, doubts and fears tried to creep back in, but Malachi and Malika held onto their unwavering faith. They repeated affirmations of self-belief and reminded themselves of their past achievements and the resilience they had demonstrated.

As they confronted their fears, something remarkable happened. They discovered that faith wasn't just a blind belief in their abilities, but a deep knowing that they had what it took to succeed. It was a trust in the process, a belief in their capacity to learn and grow, and an unwavering conviction that the universe was conspiring to support their dreams.

Armed with their newfound faith, Malachi and Malika faced their challenges head-on. They approached each experiment with confidence, knowing that failure was not a setback but an opportunity to learn and refine their approach.

Malachi and Malika realised that the principle of faith was a powerful one. It was something that could help them stay focused and motivated on their journey towards success. They knew that by developing their faith and trust in themselves and their abilities, they could overcome any obstacles and achieve their goals.

As they persevered through the ups and downs of their scientific journey, their faith grew stronger. They celebrated every small victory, knowing that each step forward brought them closer to their ultimate goal.

Their unwavering faith became a source of inspiration for others as well. Their classmates and friends noticed their resilience and began to believe in their own dreams. Malachi and Malika became role models, encouraging others to trust in themselves and pursue their passions with unwavering faith.

Activity: Building Faith

Objective: To help you develop faith in yourself and your abilities, fostering a positive mindset and resilience.

Instructions:

Faith is the belief and trust in something or someone, including yourself.

It is important to have faith in oneself as it can positively impact your life. Having faith allows you to overcome challenges, believe in your abilities, and pursue your goals with confidence.

Think about your past accomplishments and moments of success. Reflect on times when you demonstrated resilience, determination, and belief in yourself. Remind yourself of your strengths and capabilities.

Create a "Faith Journal." Get a notebook or a few sheets of paper. In this journal, you will write or draw about your achievements, positive experiences, and moments when you believed in yourself. Add to your journal regularly.

Read inspiring stories of individuals who demonstrated unwavering faith in their abilities and achieved great things. Notice the challenges they faced and how their faith helped them overcome obstacles. Understand the lessons from these stories and apply them to your own lives.

Surround yourself with positive influences. It is important to be around people who support and believe in you.

Celebrate your achievements, no matter how small, and acknowledge your efforts in developing your faith.

Remember, building faith is an ongoing process. Practice these activities regularly, faith grows stronger with time and experience. By nurturing your faith, you can develop a positive mindset, overcome obstacles, and believe in your ability to achieve your dreams.

Your Reflections

5

∽

Mind Magic: Harnessing the Power of Your Thoughts

Malachi and Malika eagerly opened the pages of 'Think and Grow Rich' to delve into the third principle: Auto-Suggestion. They knew that their beliefs and self-talk played a crucial role in shaping their path towards becoming inventors and scientists exploring the universe.

The guardian sensed their anticipation and began, "Auto-suggestion is the art of using positive affirmations and self-belief to reprogram your mind. It is the practice of consciously feeding your thoughts with empowering statements that align with your goals and desires."

Malika's eyes sparkled with curiosity. "How can auto-suggestion help us on our journey to becoming inventors and scientists exploring the universe?" she asked.

The guardian smiled, understanding her quest for knowledge. "Auto-suggestion is a powerful tool that can transform your mindset and strengthen your belief in your own abilities," he explained. "By repeating positive affirmations and visualising your success as inventors and scientists, you create a mental blueprint that propels you forward and attracts opportunities to manifest your dreams."

Malachi leaned in, his mind buzzing with possibilities. "So, by using positive affirmations and visualisations, we can program our minds to believe in our potential and overcome any obstacles?"

The guardian nodded, impressed by Malachi's insight. "Absolutely, Malachi. Auto-suggestion helps you replace self-doubt and negative thoughts with empowering beliefs. It cultivates a mindset of confidence, resilience, and unwavering faith in your abilities."

Malika couldn't help but ask, "How do we practice auto-suggestion? What are some techniques we can use?"

The guardian smiled, appreciating her eagerness to learn. "One effective technique is to create affirmations that reinforce your desired outcome. Repeat these affirmations daily, preferably in front of a mirror, and let them sink deep into your subconscious mind," he advised. "Visualise yourself as a successful scientist exploring the universe, feel the emotions of accomplishment, and let these images and feelings strengthen your belief in your own abilities."

Malachi furrowed his brow, contemplating their next steps. "Can we use auto-suggestion to overcome fear or self-doubt that may arise on our journey?"

The guardian nodded, recognising the importance of addressing such challenges. "Absolutely, Malachi. When self-doubt or fear arises, consciously replace those thoughts with positive affirmations and images of success. Remind yourself of your strengths and past achievements. This practice will help you stay focused and resilient, even in the face of challenges."

Malika's eyes sparkled with determination. "So, by using auto-suggestion, we can reprogram our minds and create a positive mindset that supports our scientific aspirations?"

The guardian nodded, a gentle smile on his face. "Indeed, Malika. Auto-suggestion empowers you to shape your reality by aligning your thoughts and beliefs with your goals. With each positive affirmation, you strengthen your confidence, attract resources, and pave the way for your success. The key to effective autosuggestion is repetition and emotion. The more you repeat your affirmations, and the more emotion you put into them, the more effective they will be in influencing your subconscious mind."

Malachi and Malika closed the book, their minds filled with the transformative potential of auto-suggestion. They knew that by harnessing the power of positive affirmations and self-belief, they were laying the foundation for their scientific greatness.

~~~~~~

Malachi and Malika had come a long way on their journey to become inventors and scientists exploring the universe. They had faced numerous challenges and overcome many obstacles, but now they found themselves confronted with a new hurdle: their own negative thoughts and limiting beliefs.

As they delved deeper into their studies, doubts began to creep into their minds. They wondered if they were truly capable of achieving their dreams. Negative thoughts whispered in their ears, telling them they weren't smart enough or talented enough to succeed.

Their wise mentor sensed their inner struggle and called them for a special meeting. He understood the power of the mind and how it could either propel them towards success or hold them back. He knew that to overcome their doubts and limiting beliefs, they needed to harness the power of auto-suggestion.

Auto-suggestion, he explained, was the process of reprogramming the subconscious mind with positive thoughts and affirmations. It involved consciously feeding their minds with empowering beliefs, replacing negative self-talk with empowering statements.

To help Malachi and Malika understand the power of auto-suggestion, their mentor guided them through a series of exercises. They were asked to write down their limiting beliefs and negative thoughts on a piece of paper. Then, with intention and determination, they tore up those papers, symbolically letting go of their self-imposed limitations.

Next, they were given a journal and instructed to write down positive affirmations and empowering statements about themselves and their abilities. They wrote phrases like "I am capable of achieving greatness," "I am a brilliant scientist," "My inventions are changing the world" and "I am deserving of success."

Every day, Malachi and Malika would read these affirmations aloud, repeating them with conviction and belief. They started to notice a shift in their mindset. The negative thoughts that had once plagued them started to lose their power. Instead, they began to embrace a positive and empowering perspective.

But auto-suggestion wasn't just about reciting affirmations. Their mentor taught them the importance of visualisation. They would close their eyes and vividly imagine themselves achieving their goals, exploring distant planets, and making ground-breaking discoveries, creating magnificent inventions. They would feel the excitement, the joy, and the sense of accomplishment as if it were happening in that very moment.

As they practiced auto-suggestion, Malachi and Malika felt a profound transformation taking place within them. The negative thoughts that had once held them back were replaced by a deep sense of self-belief and confidence. They realised that their thoughts had the power to shape their reality, and they chose to fill their minds with positive, empowering thoughts.

With their newfound belief in themselves, Malachi and Malika approached their studies with renewed enthusiasm and determination. They tackled complex scientific concepts with ease and embraced challenges as opportunities for growth. The power of auto-suggestion had unlocked their potential and propelled them towards greatness.

As time went on, Malachi and Malika saw the fruits of their auto-suggestion practice. They achieved remarkable breakthroughs in their scientific experiments and became known amongst their peers for their innovative thinking. Their classmates and teachers marvelled at their transformation, inspired by their unwavering belief in themselves.

Malachi and Malika realised that auto-suggestion was not just a technique; it was a way of life. They understood that by consciously directing their thoughts and beliefs, they had the power to shape their destiny. With auto-suggestion, they had dismantled the barriers of self-doubt and stepped into their full potential.

And so, with hearts filled with positivity and determination, Malachi and Malika embraced the power of auto-suggestion, knowing that their thoughts had the power to create a future beyond their wildest dreams.

I am capable of achieving my dreams
We can do this!
I am focused and determined to go for my goals.

Activity: Affirmations

Thinking of your goals and visions for your life, what auto-suggestions can you use to help you achieve them?

Write three to five statements that empower your mind to stay positive and take action towards your goals.

Affirmations are positive statements that can help you to reprogram your mind and change your beliefs and thought patterns. Writing affirmations can be a powerful tool for personal growth, self-improvement, and achieving your goals. Here are some instructions on how to write effective affirmations:

- Start with a clear goal: Before you begin writing affirmations, it's important to know what you want to achieve. Think about the specific goal or outcome you want to manifest, and make sure it's something that's meaningful to you.

- Write in the present tense, future tense or natural (tense): Affirmations should be written in the present tense, future tense or natural, as if the desired outcome has already happened. For example, "I am successful", "I will be successful by this time next year", "The ability to succeed is within me". Choose the tense that resonates with you and feels believable as you repeat it. Natural tense affirmations are easily and readily accepted by your conscious and subconscious mind as your truth.

- Use positive language: Affirmations should always be framed in positive language. Avoid using negative words like "don't," "can't," or "won't," as these can reinforce negative beliefs and thought patterns. Instead, focus on what you want to achieve and use positive words to describe it.

- Keep it simple: Affirmations should be short, simple, and easy to remember. Avoid using complex or convoluted language, and stick to simple, straightforward statements that clearly express your desired outcome.

- Make it personal and specific: Your affirmations should be specific to you and your goals. Use language that resonates with you and reflects your personal beliefs and values. Set time frames on future tense affirmations - "I will be successful by 25 years old".

- Repeat regularly: To make affirmations effective, you need to repeat them regularly. Set aside a specific time each day to repeat your affirmations, and say them out loud if possible. This helps to reinforce the message and create a stronger belief in your desired outcome.

Remember that affirmations are a tool to help you shift your mindset and beliefs, but they are not a magic solution. To achieve your goals, you also need to take action and make changes in your life. Use affirmations as a tool to support your personal growth and development, and remember to be patient and kind to yourself as you work towards your goals.

6

⌣

The Secrets Unveiled: Opening Your Treasure Bank

Malachi and Malika eagerly turned the pages of 'Think and Grow Rich' to unveil the fourth principle: Specialised Knowledge. They knew that to become inventors and scientists exploring the universe, they needed to equip themselves with the right knowledge and expertise.

The guardian, noticing their enthusiasm, began, "Specialised knowledge is the key that unlocks the door to success. It is the deep understanding and expertise in a specific field that sets you apart and propels you toward your goals."

Malachi leaned forward, eager to grasp the concept. "So, what kind of specialised knowledge do we need to become scientists exploring the universe?" he asked.

The guardian smiled, appreciating Malachi's curiosity. "To explore the universe, you will need a solid foundation in subjects like physics, astronomy, mathematics, and other scientific disciplines," he explained.

"You must immerse yourself in learning and continuously seek to expand your knowledge in these areas."

Malika nodded, her eyes gleaming. "So, it's important to study and acquire knowledge in our chosen field to become experts?"

The guardian nodded in agreement. "Absolutely, Malika. As you acquire specialised knowledge, you will gain a deeper understanding of the universe and develop unique insights. This knowledge will empower you to make significant contributions to the scientific community."

Malachi furrowed his brow, contemplating their next steps. "But where do we find specialised knowledge? How do we learn and acquire it?"

The guardian nodded approvingly. "Excellent questions, Malachi. Specialised knowledge can be obtained through various sources. Books, online resources, educational institutions, and mentorship are all valuable avenues to acquire the knowledge you seek."

Malika raised her hand, eager to learn more. "Are there any specific activities or habits that can help us accelerate our learning and acquisition of specialised knowledge?"

The guardian smiled, recognising Malika's hunger for knowledge. "Certainly, Malika. Engage in activities like conducting experiments, participating in science fairs, attending lectures, and joining scientific clubs or communities. These experiences will provide you with practical knowledge and opportunities to collaborate with like-minded individuals."

Malachi leaned in, his excitement palpable. "So, by actively seeking specialised knowledge and immersing ourselves in the subject matter, we can become experts in our chosen field?"

The guardian nodded, a twinkle in his eyes. "Indeed, Malachi. By investing time and effort into acquiring specialised knowledge, you position yourself as a valuable resource in the scientific realm. Your expertise will open doors and enable you to make significant contributions."

Malachi and Malika exchanged determined glances, knowing that acquiring specialised knowledge was the key to unlocking their potential as inventors and scientists exploring the universe.

The guardian concluded, "Remember, my young seekers, specialised knowledge is a lifelong pursuit. Embrace learning with curiosity and passion. Continuously seek to expand your knowledge, and let it guide you on your journey to greatness."

Malachi and Malika closed the book, their minds buzzing with the possibilities that lay ahead. They understood that by acquiring specialised knowledge, they would become unstoppable in their pursuit of exploring the universe.

~~~~~~

Excitement filled the air as Malachi and Malika delved into the world of specialised knowledge, the fourth principle on their journey towards becoming inventors and scientists exploring the universe. Their wise mentor knew that to truly excel in their chosen fields, they needed to acquire in-depth knowledge and expertise.

The mentor started by introducing them to various experts and professionals in the scientific community. Together, they embarked on a thrilling quest to gather knowledge and uncover hidden secrets. Their journey took them to laboratories, observatories, and research centres, where they had the opportunity to meet brilliant minds who shared their wisdom and experiences.

Their first stop was the Space Research Centre, where they met Dr. Thompson, a renowned astrophysicist. Dr. Thompson took them on a mesmerising tour, explaining the wonders of the universe and the mysteries waiting to be unravelled. Malachi and Malika listened with rapt attention, absorbing every word like sponges.

Next, they visited the Robotics Institute, where they met Professor Rodriguez, an expert in robotics and artificial intelligence. Professor Rodriguez introduced them to cutting-edge technology and demonstrated how robots could assist in space exploration. Malachi and Malika were in awe as they witnessed robots manoeuvring with precision and performing complex tasks.

Their journey also led them to the Deep Sea Exploration Centre, where they met Dr. Chen, a marine biologist. Dr. Chen shared her passion for the mysteries of the deep sea and the incredible creatures that dwell in its depths. Malachi and Malika were captivated by her stories and the amazing photographs she had taken during her expeditions.

As they met experts from different fields, Malachi and Malika realised the importance of specialised knowledge. They saw how these experts had dedicated their lives to acquiring expertise in their respective fields and how it had propelled them to great achievements.

Inspired by their encounters, Malachi and Malika sought ways to acquire specialised knowledge themselves. They spent hours at the library, poring over books and scientific journals, eager to deepen their understanding of the universe. They also attended workshops and seminars, engaging in hands-on experiments and discussions with fellow aspiring inventors and scientists.

In addition to formal learning, their mentor encouraged them to explore unconventional sources of knowledge. They interviewed astronauts, watched documentaries, and even embarked on stargazing adventures, immersing themselves in the wonders of the cosmos.

Along their journey, Malachi and Malika discovered that acquiring specialised knowledge was not just about memorising facts and figures. It was about understanding the underlying principles, developing critical thinking skills, and continuously expanding their horizons.

As their quest for specialised knowledge continued, Malachi and Malika grew in confidence and competence. They became familiar with scientific concepts and theories, applying their knowledge to solve complex problems and engage in insightful discussions. Their dedication and thirst for knowledge set them apart, earning them the respect and admiration of their mentors and peers.

With each step on their journey, Malachi and Malika realised that the acquisition of specialised knowledge was not a destination but a lifelong pursuit. They understood that the more they learned, the more they discovered how much there was still to explore.

Armed with newfound knowledge and a hunger for discovery, Malachi and Malika continued their adventure, eager to unlock the secrets of the universe. They knew that specialised knowledge would be their guiding light, illuminating the path to their dreams.

Activity: Acquire specialised knowledge on your goals.

- The first step is to choose the goal that you desire to achieve. It could be anything from space to animals to technology. Choose something that you're excited learning more about.

- Research: Once you know your goal, start researching it. You can use books, websites, videos, and other resources to gather information. Make notes, write down any questions you have.

- Talk to experts: Look for experts in your chosen field and reach out to them. You can email or message them on social media and ask them questions about their work. Most experts are happy to share their knowledge with curious kids.

- Experiment and observe: Depending on the topic you've chosen, you may be able to conduct experiments or make observations to learn more. For example, if you're interested in animals, you could set up a bird feeder and observe the different species that come to eat.

- Attend workshops or classes: Look for workshops or classes in your area that relate to your topic. You can learn a lot from experienced teachers and other students who share your interest.

- Create a project: Once you've gathered all your knowledge, it's time to create a project. You could create a presentation, write a report, or even make a video. Share your project with friends and family, and you might inspire others to learn about your chosen topic too.

Remember, acquiring specialised knowledge takes time and effort, but it's also a lot of fun. By following these steps, you can become an expert in any field you choose!

Your Reflections

7

∽

The Wonders Within: The Attraction of Your Imagination

Excitement filled the air as Malachi and Malika turned to Chapter 6 in 'Think and Grow Rich', eager to explore the power of imagination. They knew that their dreams of becoming inventors and scientists exploring the universe would be fuelled by the creative and boundless realm of their imagination.

The guardian noticed their anticipation and smiled warmly. "Imagination is the magical force that allows you to envision possibilities beyond what currently exists," he began. "It is the spark that ignites innovation and allows you to dream big."

Malika's eyes sparkled with curiosity. "How does imagination help us become inventors and scientists exploring the universe?" she asked.

The guardian nodded, understanding her quest for knowledge. "Imagination helps you to visualise the wonders of the universe, to see yourself conducting ground-breaking experiments, creating innovative inventions, and to envision the discoveries waiting to be made," he explained.

"It is through the power of your imagination that you tap into your creative potential and unlock new pathways of scientific exploration."

Malachi leaned forward, his mind buzzing with ideas. "So, we need to use our imagination to think beyond what we already know, to dream up new possibilities?"

The guardian nodded, impressed by Malachi's perceptiveness. "Absolutely, Malachi. Imagination allows you to push the boundaries of what is known and explore uncharted territories. It enables you to think outside the box and consider new and creative ways to solve problems. By using your imagination, you can come up with innovative solutions to challenges that might have otherwise seemed impossible to overcome and conceive ground-breaking ideas that can change the world."

Malika couldn't contain her excitement. "But how do we harness the power of imagination? How do we strengthen it?"

The guardian smiled, sensing her eagerness to learn. "Imagination is like a muscle that grows stronger with exercise," he explained. "Engage in activities that stimulate your creativity, such as drawing, writing, storytelling, and even daydreaming. Allow your mind to wander and explore the infinite possibilities that lie within."

Malachi furrowed his brow, contemplating their next steps. "So, by nurturing our imagination, we can come up with innovative solutions to the challenges we may face as scientists and inventors?"

The guardian nodded, impressed by Malachi's grasp of the concept. "Exactly, Malachi. Imagination fuels problem-solving and helps you see obstacles as opportunities for innovation. Embrace your imagination as a powerful tool in your scientific journey."

Malika couldn't help but ask, "Is there anything else we can do to strengthen our imagination?"

The guardian nodded approvingly. "Immerse yourself in literature, science fiction, and documentaries. Explore different perspectives and ideas from various cultures and time periods. Expand your knowledge and feed your imagination with a rich tapestry of experiences and information."

Malachi and Malika exchanged excited glances, realising that their imagination held the key to unlocking a universe of possibilities.

The guardian concluded, "Remember, my young seekers, imagination is the bridge between your dreams and their manifestation. Nurture it, let it soar, and watch as it leads you to new frontiers of scientific exploration."

Malachi and Malika closed the book, their minds bustling with the endless potential their imagination held. They knew that by embracing the power of their imagination, they were one step closer to realising their dreams of becoming inventors and scientists exploring the universe.

~~~~~~

In a hidden corner of the mentor's abode, nestled among shelves filled with ancient books and mysterious artifacts, stood a magical workshop. This was the place where Malachi and Malika would unlock the incredible power of their imaginations, the fifth principle on their journey towards becoming inventors and scientists exploring the universe.

As they entered the workshop, a sense of wonder cloaked them. The air crackled with electricity, and shelves were adorned with colourful jars containing swirling mists of dreams and ideas. In the centre of the room, a large table stood, covered with parchment, paintbrushes, and an assortment of art supplies.

Their mentor explained that the power of imagination was like a gateway to a world of infinite possibilities. It allowed them to visualise their dreams and explore the depths of their creativity. The workshop was a place where they could tap into this power and harness it for their journey ahead.

With wide-eyed anticipation, Malachi and Malika eagerly began their exploration. The mentor guided them through various exercises and activities designed to unleash their imaginations. They started with simple visualisation exercises, closing their eyes and picturing themselves as inventors and scientists, floating through space, discovering new galaxies, and unravelling cosmic mysteries.

As they practiced, they noticed the power of their thoughts. They could see, hear, and feel the vivid details of their imagined experiences. The mentor encouraged them to embrace this visualisation technique in their daily lives, using it to strengthen their belief in their goals and dreams.

Next, they turned to creative expression. The mentor provided them with sketchbooks, paints, and clay, inviting them to give form to their imagination. Malachi and Malika unleashed their inner artists, painting vivid landscapes of distant planets, sculpting intricate models of spacecraft, drawing innovative new inventions, and creating imaginative illustrations of the wonders of the universe.

Through their creative endeavours, they discovered that the act of bringing their imagination to life amplified its power. As they crafted their visions, they infused them with their emotions, hopes, and aspirations, breathing life into their dreams.

In the workshop, Malachi and Malika also learned the importance of thinking outside the box. They engaged in brainstorming sessions, where they generated innovative ideas and solutions to scientific challenges. The mentor encouraged them to embrace unconventional thinking, to question assumptions, and to explore uncharted territories of knowledge.

In these sessions, the boundaries of their imagination expanded. They realised that there were no limits to what they could conceive and create. They began to see challenges as opportunities for innovative thinking and problem-solving, opening up new pathways for their scientific explorations.

As their time in the workshop came to an end, Malachi and Malika felt a profound sense of empowerment. They had unlocked the incredible power of their imaginations and understood that their thoughts and ideas held the key to shaping their reality. They realised that imagination was not just a whimsical notion but a force that could propel them towards their dreams.

Leaving the magical workshop, Malachi and Malika carried the essence of their newfound power within them. They knew that in their pursuit of becoming inventors and scientists exploring the universe, their imagination would be their constant companion, guiding them through the uncharted realms of scientific discovery.

With souls full of imagination, and minds brimming with creative possibilities, Malachi and Malika stepped forward, ready to conquer the unknown and make their dreams a reality.

Activity: Activate your Imagination

How to use your imagination effectively.

One way to do this is by guided visualisation exercises.

These exercises can help you visualise your goals and dreams and create a mental image of what you want to achieve. They can also help you build your self-confidence and overcome fears and doubts.

For example, you can guide yourself through a visualisation exercise where you imagine yourself achieving your goals. Close your eyes and picture yourself accomplishing something you have always wanted to do. Imagine all the details, such as how you feel, what you see, and what you hear. Imagine any obstacles you might encounter and how you would overcome them.

Use your imagination to solve problems.

- When you encounter a challenge or obstacle, come up with creative solutions using your imagination. For example, if you are struggling with a difficult math problem, imagine a real-life situation where you might need to use that skill. This can help you see the relevance of what you are learning and find creative ways to solve the problem.

- Develop your imagination through storytelling. Stories provide us with a rich source of imagery and ideas that can stimulate our imagination and spark our creativity. When we hear stories, we can picture the characters, settings, and events in our minds, which can help us develop our visualisation skills.

- Spark your imagination through creative activities such as drawing, painting, and writing. These activities allow us to express our thoughts and ideas in a visual or written form and to explore different possibilities and perspectives.

- When you visualise yourself succeeding in your goals, you build a positive image of yourself, which can boost your self-confidence and motivate you to take action.

- Your imagination is a powerful tool that can help you achieve your goals, but it must be combined with action. Take small steps towards your goals every day, and remember that persistence and hard work are also necessary to turn your imagination into reality.

8

∾

Blueprint for Success: Building Your Path to Greatness

Malachi and Malika eagerly turned to Chapter 7 in 'Think and Grow Rich', ready to uncover the secrets of organised planning. They knew that to fulfil their dreams of becoming scientists and inventors, they needed a well-structured and strategic approach.

The guardian noticed their excitement and began, "Organised planning is the art of creating a detailed roadmap to guide you towards your goals. It involves breaking down your big vision into smaller, actionable steps and outlining a clear strategy to achieve them."

Malika's eyes widened with anticipation. "How can organised planning help us on our journey to becoming inventors and scientists exploring the universe?" she asked.

The guardian smiled, recognising her eagerness for knowledge. "Organised planning helps you transform your dreams into achievable goals," he explained. "By mapping out the necessary actions, allocating resources effectively, and establishing a timeline, you set yourself up for success and navigate the path towards scientific greatness."

Malachi leaned forward, his mind lively with possibilities. "So, by planning our steps and creating a roadmap, we can make progress towards our ultimate goal?"

The guardian nodded, impressed by Malachi's understanding. "Absolutely, Malachi. Organised planning provides clarity and direction. It helps you stay focused, prioritise your actions, and make informed decisions that propel you closer to your destination."

Malika couldn't contain her enthusiasm. "How do we create an organised plan? What are the key elements we should consider?"

The guardian smiled, knowing the importance of a well-structured plan. "Start by clearly defining your ultimate goal of becoming inventors and scientists exploring the universe. Break it down into smaller, manageable milestones," he advised. "Then, identify the necessary actions, skills, and resources needed to accomplish each milestone. Anticipate potential obstacles and develop strategies to overcome them. It is important to think through different scenarios and developing contingency plans, in case things do not go exactly as expected. Celebrate small wins along the way and use those victories as motivation to keep moving forward."

Malachi furrowed his brow, contemplating their next steps. "What about collaboration? Should we include others in our organised plan?"

The guardian nodded, acknowledging the value of collaboration. "Absolutely, Malachi. Collaborating with like-minded individuals who share your vision can amplify your efforts and bring fresh perspectives. Surround yourselves with a mastermind group that supports your goals and fosters a collective mindset of growth and success."

Malika nodded, absorbing the wisdom. "So, by creating an organised plan, we can stay focused, take consistent action, and adapt when necessary?"

The guardian smiled, proud of their grasp of the concept. "Indeed, Malika. Organised planning empowers you to be proactive, efficient, and adaptable. It sets you up for success and maximises your chances of achieving your dreams."

Malachi and Malika closed the book, their minds vibrant with excitement. They understood that by implementing organised planning, they were laying the groundwork for their scientific journey through the vast universe.

~~~~~~

As Malachi and Malika continued their journey towards becoming inventors and scientists exploring the universe, they encountered a familiar feeling creeping in: overwhelm. Their dreams seemed grand, their goals immense, and the path ahead felt daunting. The weight of their ambitions threatened to engulf them.

Sensing their unease, their mentor knew it was time to activate the power of organised planning, the sixth principle of their quest. In a cosy study filled with books, charts, and maps, the mentor began explaining the importance of breaking down their goals into manageable steps and creating a roadmap to success.

The mentor shared stories of renowned explorers who conquered vast territories and achieved extraordinary feats through meticulous planning. They emphasised that success was not just a product of dreams and aspirations but required a clear strategy and a well-thought-out plan.

To illustrate the concept, the mentor provided Malachi and Malika with large sheets of paper and colourful markers. They were encouraged to write down their ultimate goal at the top of the page and then break it down into smaller, more achievable tasks. Each task represented a step forward on their journey.

Malachi and Malika eagerly began their planning process. They brainstormed the various aspects of their goal, identified the skills they needed to acquire, and listed the resources and support they would require along the way. They plotted milestones, creating a timeline that showcased the progression of their efforts.

As they filled the sheets with their plans, the overwhelming nature of their goals began to subside. They realised that by breaking them down into smaller tasks, they could approach them one step at a time. The mentor reminded them that even the most colossal achievements were the result of consistent effort and focused actions.

In the following days, Malachi and Malika found solace in their organised plans. Each morning, they reviewed their roadmap, selecting the tasks they would tackle that day. They set aside dedicated time for study, research, and experimentation, ensuring that they made progress towards their dreams.

With their goals broken down into manageable chunks, Malachi and Malika found a renewed sense of focus and purpose. They discovered that organised planning not only alleviated overwhelm but also provided a sense of direction and clarity. It gave them a roadmap to follow, guiding them through the vast expanse of their aspirations.

But the mentor reminded them that plans were not set in stone. Life was full of surprises and unexpected turns, and flexibility was key. He encouraged Malachi and Malika to adapt their plans as needed, to remain open to new opportunities, and to embrace change when it served their purpose.

As the days turned into weeks and weeks into months, Malachi and Malika witnessed the power of their organised planning. They saw their progress unfold, their dreams inch closer, and their confidence grow. The once overwhelming path now felt more manageable, and they felt empowered by their ability to chart their course.

With their roadmap as their guide, Malachi and Malika embarked on each day with purpose and determination. They knew that success was not just a distant destination but a series of deliberate steps taken in the present moment. They understood that by organising their efforts, they could navigate even the most complex challenges and turn their dreams into reality.

And so, armed with their plans, their dreams, and a deep sense of purpose, Malachi and Malika continued their journey towards becoming inventors and scientists exploring the universe. With each step, they knew they were inching closer to the stars, guided by the power of organised planning and fuelled by their unwavering determination.

Activity: Set SMART goals

- Specific
- Measurable
- Achievable
- Realistic
- Time bound

By using the SMART system in choosing your goals, can increase your success rate from 3% to as much as 90%.

SMART goals offer you a pathway of action.

A clear pattern for formulating a goal with small and manageable steps that will reach your target.

Begin by breaking your vision down into manageable pieces to plan your actions.
This provides a structure in which to guide you as you work.

Many people don't reach their goals because they give up at the first hurdle, as soon as things start to go wrong.

This is brought about primarily by a lack of self-belief and low self-esteem.

However, those that believe they can from the start do not quit at the first sign of trouble, as they believe that they can do it, they persevere and find another way to get over or around the hurdle!

They make mistakes, but they learn from them and keep on trying different ways until they succeed.

They do not give up!

Plan your actions!

Small measurable steps that builds to success!

Take Inspired Action

When we take the time to really think about what we are doing, to visualise ourselves being and doing our goal successfully, we often become clear/see the path that we need to take to achieve it.

Things we didn't see before suddenly become clear as the path to take.

This is Inspired Action!

VIBE into Action

- Visualise
- Intention
- Belief
- Expectation

Take some quiet time and Visualise yourself doing / being your goal successfully.Set your Intention of what you want to achieve. Believe that it will manifest itself and have the Expectation to see your goal to completion.

Inspired Action produces inspired results that move you closer to achieving your goals.

VIBE into Action

Your Reflections

9

〜

The Power of Choice: Paving Your Way to Adventure

Malachi and Malika turned to the next chapter of 'Think and Grow Rich', eager to unlock the power of decision-making. They knew that to achieve their dreams of becoming scientists and inventors, they needed to make firm and unwavering decisions.

The guardian noticed their anticipation and began, "The seventh principle, my young friends, is Decision. It is the act of making definitive choices and committing yourself wholeheartedly to the path you have chosen."

Malika's eyes sparkled with curiosity. "How does decision-making help us on our journey to becoming scientists exploring the universe?" she asked.

The guardian smiled, understanding her inquiring mind. "Decisions are the building blocks of progress," he explained. "When you make a firm decision, you create a clear direction for your actions. It eliminates doubt and allows you to channel your energy towards achieving your goals."

Malachi leaned in, his mind active with possibilities. "So, by making strong decisions, we can overcome indecision and take focused action towards our dreams?"

The guardian nodded, impressed by Malachi's awareness. "Exactly, Malachi. Decisiveness empowers you to move forward with conviction. It eliminates the wavering and second-guessing that can hinder your progress."

Malachi realised that many people struggle with making decisions. They get stuck in indecision, in analysis paralysis, weighing the pros and cons without ever actually taking any action. But he knew that successful people were different. They made clear and confident decisions, and they followed through on them.

Malika couldn't help but ask, "But what if we make the wrong decision? How can we ensure we choose the right path?"

The guardian's eyes twinkled with wisdom. "In life, there are no guarantees, my dear Malika," he replied. "However, making a decision, even if it turns out to be the wrong one, is better than being paralysed by indecision. Learn from any missteps, adjust your course if necessary, and continue moving forward."

Malachi furrowed his brow, contemplating their next steps. "How can we strengthen our decision-making skills? Are there any techniques we can use?"

The guardian nodded, appreciating his quest for self-improvement. "One powerful technique is to gather all the relevant information about the choices before you," he advised. "Consider the potential outcomes, weigh the pros and cons, and trust your intuition. Listen to your inner voice, for it often holds the wisdom you seek."

Malika's eyes lit up with determination. "So, by making firm decisions, we can align our actions with our goals and overcome the challenges that come our way?"

The guardian nodded, a gentle smile on his face. "Indeed, Malika. Decisions propel you forward on your journey. They ignite your inner fire, fuel your determination, and give you the strength to persevere."

Malachi and Malika closed the book, their minds filled with the transformative power of decision-making. They understood that by making decisive choices and staying true to their path, they were paving the way for their scientific greatness.

~~~~~~~~~~~~~~~~~~~~~~~~~~~~~~~~~~~~

As Malachi and Malika ventured further into their scientific journey, they reached another crucial crossroad. They found themselves standing at the intersection of possibilities, where important decisions about their future awaited them. It was a moment that called for deep introspection and the art of decisive thinking.

Sensing their contemplation, the mentor called them together for a special session. He presented them with a series of thought-provoking exercises and guided discussions to help them explore their passions, values, and aspirations.

The first exercise involved creating a vision board. Malachi and Malika gathered images, quotes, and symbols that represented their dreams and goals. As they arranged the pieces on their boards, they visualised their desired future, letting their imaginations soar. This exercise helped them clarify their aspirations and reminded them of the possibilities that lay ahead.

Next, the mentor engaged them in a reflective conversation. He encouraged them to delve deep into their hearts and souls, asking thought-provoking questions about their interests, strengths, and the impact they wished to make in the world.

Malachi and Malika shared their innermost desires, expressing their fascination with the mysteries of the universe, innovative inventions, and their deep desire to contribute to scientific knowledge, exploration and invention. They spoke of their eagerness to inspire others and ignite a passion for discovery.

With each passing conversation, the path ahead became clearer. The mentor guided them in exploring different educational opportunities, research institutes, and scientific communities that aligned with their aspirations. They researched renowned scientists and their ground-breaking discoveries, drawing inspiration from their journeys.

The mentor encouraged them to seek advice from experts in the field and to connect with mentors who could offer guidance and support. They attended science conferences, participated in workshops, and engaged in collaborative projects with other aspiring scientists and inventors. These experiences provided them with invaluable insights and expanded their understanding of the scientific community.

Through these exercises and discussions, Malachi and Malika began to understand the importance of decisive thinking. They realised that making choices aligned with their true passions and values would enable them to live a life of purpose and fulfilment.

In a moment of deep reflection, Malachi and Malika made their decisions. They committed themselves wholeheartedly to the path of scientific innovative exploration. They acknowledged the challenges that lay ahead and the sacrifices they would have to make, but their determination remained unwavering.

With their decisions made, Malachi and Malika felt a sense of clarity and purpose wash over them. They knew that they were embarking on a lifelong journey of scientific discovery, and they were ready to face whatever challenges awaited them.

The mentor, observing their resolute expressions, smiled with pride. "Decisiveness is the key to unlocking your full potential," he said. "When you commit to your chosen path with unwavering determination, the universe conspires to support you."

With a renewed sense of purpose, Malachi and Malika embraced their decisions and set forth on their chosen paths, ready to face the adventures and discoveries that awaited them.

And so, with the power of decisive thinking guiding their steps, they embarked on a new chapter of their scientific journey, knowing that they were walking the path they were meant to tread.

Activity: Who's your Role Model?

Is there someone who has already done what you want to do?

- What if you could do what they did?
- We do not have to re-invent the wheel when we can model some-one else's actions.
- Who has achieved your desires? Who's your role model?
- Find someone who has already achieved your goal and research them.
- What did they do achieve their goal?
- What steps did they take?
- What was their mindset?
- What were they thinking?
- What hurdles did they face?
- How did they overcome their hurdles?
- How do they inspire you?

When you research your role model, you will find beneath it all, the one key element that sets successful achievers apart from the others.

Self-Belief

They ultimately believed that they could do it and didn't stop until they did.

They took inspired action and manifested their desires, goals and aspirations to become successful in their lives.

Some started their journey when they were young children, some later in life, but the belief in self was always there, whether they knew it or not!

BELIEVE IN YOURSELF and your abilities to succeed in your true desires.

Celebrate the small victories that lead on to bigger successes.

Build **SELF BELIEF**

10

༄

Keep Going, Never Quit: Your Inner Determination

Malachi and Malika eagerly delved into Chapter 9 of 'Think and Grow Rich', ready to uncover the secrets of persistence. They knew that to achieve their dreams of becoming inventors and scientists exploring the universe, they needed unwavering perseverance.

The guardian observed their excitement and began, "Persistence is the fuel that keeps you going even when faced with challenges or setbacks. It is the unwavering determination to continue striving towards your goals, no matter what obstacles may arise."

Malika's eyes gleamed with grit. "How does persistence help us on our journey to becoming inventors and scientists exploring the universe?" she asked eagerly.

The guardian smiled, acknowledging her determination. "Persistence is what separates those who give up from those who achieve greatness," he explained. "In the face of difficulties, it is the inner strength that allows you to stay committed, adapt, and push through obstacles to reach your desired destination even when it feels like there's no end in sight."

Malachi leaned forward, his mind racing with probabilities. "So, by being persistent, we can overcome challenges and keep moving forward on our path to scientific invention and exploration?"

The guardian nodded, impressed by Malachi's understanding. "Indeed, Malachi. Persistence helps you develop resilience and perseverance. It enables you to learn from failures, adapt your strategies, and continue taking inspired action."

Malika couldn't help but ask, "But what if we encounter setbacks or obstacles that seem unbeatable? How can we stay persistent?"

The guardian's eyes sparkled with wisdom. "Remember, my dear Malika, setbacks are part of the journey," he reassured her. "Embrace them as opportunities for growth. It is important to have a growth mindset. Instead of getting discouraged when things get tough, view challenges as opportunities to learn and grow. Every mistake is a chance to improve and get better. Stay focused on your vision and remind yourself of the reasons behind your pursuit. Seek support from mentors and surround yourself with a supportive community who will uplift and encourage you during challenging times."

Malachi wrinkled his brow, contemplating their next steps. "Are there any techniques or practices that can help us cultivate persistence?"

The guardian nodded, appreciating his desire to know more. "One technique is to break down your goals into smaller, manageable steps," he suggested. "Celebrate your progress along the way, and use setbacks as stepping stones to learn and improve. Stay disciplined, maintain a positive mindset, and develop daily habits that keep you focused and motivated."

Malika's resolve shone brightly. "So, by embracing persistence, we can overcome any obstacles and continue on our path towards scientific exploration of the universe?"

The guardian smiled, his heart filled with pride. "Absolutely, Malika. Persistence is the key that unlocks the doors to success. It is the unwavering commitment to your dreams and the willingness to keep going, even when the path seems challenging."

Malachi and Malika closed the book, their hearts filled with the power of persistence. They understood that by staying persistent, they were equipped to overcome any obstacles and reach the stars in their pursuit of scientific greatness.

~~~~~~

As Malachi and Malika continued their journey of exploration and growth, they encountered obstacles and setbacks that tested their determination. But with the guidance of their wise mentor, they learned the power of unwavering persistence and resilience.

One day, as they embarked on a particularly challenging experiment, Malachi's experiment failed, causing frustration to well up inside him. Doubts crept into his mind, and he questioned whether he was truly capable of achieving his dream of becoming a renowned inventor.

Malika, noticing her friend's discouragement, approached him with a reassuring smile. "Remember, Malachi, setbacks are a part of the journey. They help us learn and grow stronger," she reminded him.

Their mentor, observing their interaction, joined in. "Indeed, setbacks are not indicators of failure but opportunities for growth," he said. "It is in the face of challenges that our true character and determination are tested. It is when we refuse to give up that we grow stronger and closer to our goals."

Malachi took a deep breath and nodded, determined to overcome his doubts. "You're right," he said, his voice filled with renewed fortitude. "I won't let this setback define me. I will learn from it and keep pushing forward."

With their mentor's guidance, Malachi and Malika developed a steadfast resolve to overcome any obstacle they encountered. They recognised that setbacks were merely stepping stones to success, and they approached each challenge with renewed vigour.

They studied diligently, sought advice from experts in the field, and embraced a growth mindset that allowed them to see setbacks as opportunities for improvement. They learned from their mistakes, refined their techniques, and developed new strategies to overcome obstacles.

As time went on, their persistence began to pay off. They celebrated small victories along the way, each success fuelling their purpose to continue their pursuit of innovative scientific exploration.

But their journey was not without its share of trials. There were moments when it seemed as though the universe conspired against them, throwing one obstacle after another in their path. Yet, they remained steadfast in their commitment, refusing to give up on their dreams.

The mentor watched with pride as Malachi and Malika faced these challenges head-on, demonstrating unwavering persistence and resilience. He knew that this was a vital lesson in their journey, one that would shape them into the remarkable scientists and inventors they aspired to be.

Finally, after months of perseverance, they achieved a breakthrough.

Their experiment yielded remarkable results, leaving them awestruck at the wonders of the universe they had uncovered.

Activity: Tracking Progress

- Get a chart or a journal where you can track your progress. Record your achievements, no matter how small, and celebrate your successes. This will reinforce the idea that persistence pays off.

- **Facing Challenges:** Setbacks and challenges are a natural part of any journey.
- Anticipate potential obstacles and brainstorm strategies to overcome them.
- Approach challenges with a positive mindset and to see them as opportunities for growth.

- **Learning from Mistakes:** View failures as valuable learning experiences and identify what you can do differently next time. Setbacks are not permanent, but stepping stones towards improvement.

- **Support Network:** Seeking support and guidance when faced with difficulties.
- Reach out to trusted adults, mentors, or friends who can provide encouragement and advice. Stay motivated and persevere.

- **Visualisation and Affirmations:** Visualise yourself achieving your goal and repeat positive statements related to your persistence and determination. This will reinforce your belief in yourself and your ability to overcome obstacles.

- **Celebrate Milestones:** celebrate your accomplishment.

- Recognise your efforts, whether it's with a small reward, a special treat, or simply a heartfelt acknowledgment. This will motivate you to keep going and reinforce the importance of persistence.

- **Role Models and Stories:** Read stories of famous individuals who demonstrated persistence in achieving their goals. Talk about their struggles and how they persevered despite setbacks. This will inspire you and help you understand that even successful people face challenges, but it's their persistence that sets them apart.

By engaging in this activity, you will learn the value of persistence and develop the mindset necessary to overcome obstacles. You will understand that success often requires sustained effort and that setbacks are merely opportunities for growth. Implementing the principle of persistence will equip you with the resilience and determination needed to reach your goals.

Your Reflections

11

～

Dream Team Unite: The Superpowers of Collaboration

Malachi and Malika eagerly turned to Chapter 10 of 'Think and Grow Rich', ready to unravel the secrets of the power of the mastermind. They knew that collaboration and synergy were essential in their journey to becoming inventors and scientists exploring the universe.

The guardian noticed their keenness and began, "The ninth principle is the Power of the Mastermind. It is the idea that when two or more minds come together in harmony, a greater force is created."

Malika's eyes sparkled with curiosity. "How does the power of the mastermind help us on our path to becoming scientists and inventors?" she asked.

The guardian smiled, understanding her inquisitiveness. "The power of the mastermind allows you to tap into the collective intelligence, experience, and creativity of a group. It amplifies your ideas, opens doors to new possibilities, and accelerates your progress towards your goals. This principle emphasises the importance of surrounding yourself with a group of like-minded individuals who are committed to achieving their goals. A Mastermind can be incredibly powerful because it allows everyone to tap into the collective knowledge, experience, and resources of the group."

Malachi jumped up, his mind bubbling with excitement. "So, by collaborating with others who share our passion for inventing and scientific exploration, we can achieve more than we could on our own?"

The guardian nodded, impressed by Malachi's understanding. "Exactly, Malachi. When minds come together, they create a synergy that surpasses individual capabilities. It is a meeting of diverse perspectives and skills that can lead to breakthroughs and innovative solutions."

Malika couldn't help but ask, "How do we harness the power of the mastermind? How do we find like-minded individuals to collaborate with?"

The guardian's eyes twinkled with wisdom. "Finding a mastermind group starts with identifying individuals who share similar goals, passions, and values," he explained. "Reach out to scientists, inventors, researchers, and other young enthusiasts who are eager to explore the wonders of the universe and creation. Attend workshops, conferences, or join online communities where you can connect with like-minded individuals."

Malachi scratched his head, contemplating their next steps. "Are there any techniques or practices that can help us maximise the power of the mastermind?"

The guardian nodded. "Active participation, effective communication, and an open mind are essential in harnessing the power of the mastermind," he advised. "Listen to others, contribute your ideas, and be receptive to feedback. Embrace collaboration as a means to learn, grow, and achieve greatness together."

Malika was excited "So, by embracing the power of the mastermind, we can tap into the collective wisdom and propel our scientific exploration of the universe?"

The guardian smiled, his heart filled with pride. "Absolutely, Malika. The power of the mastermind can fuel your journey, connect you with mentors and experts, and provide invaluable support and guidance. Together, you can unlock the mysteries of the universe and make extraordinary discoveries."

Malachi and Malika closed the book, their minds singing with the power of collaboration. They understood that by harnessing the power of the mastermind, they could reach new heights in their innovative scientific pursuits.

~~~~~~

As Malachi and Malika ventured further on their quest to become inventors and scientists exploring the universe, they began to realise the immense power of collaboration. Their mentor had taught them about the ninth principle: the power of the mastermind. They understood that by surrounding themselves with like-minded individuals, they could amplify their efforts and achieve extraordinary results.

Excitement filled the air as Malachi and Malika set out to find their fellow dreamers, eager to form an unstoppable mastermind alliance. They sought out individuals who shared their passion for the mysteries of the universe, innovative invention creation, and the pursuit of scientific knowledge. They wanted to connect with those who would uplift and support their ambitions.

Word spread quickly, and soon enough, a group of young aspiring scientists and inventors gathered together in a cosy meeting space. There, they introduced themselves, sharing their dreams, aspirations, and the challenges they faced on their individual paths. The room hummed with energy as ideas were exchanged, and the seeds of collaboration were sown.

Guided by their mentor, Malachi and Malika led the group in a series of collaborative activities. They brainstormed ideas, shared their knowledge, and offered support and encouragement. They realised that each member possessed unique talents, skills, and perspectives that, when combined, created a synergy that surpassed anything they could achieve alone.

The mastermind alliance became a place of inspiration and growth. Each member contributed their expertise, pushing the boundaries of their collective knowledge. They celebrated each other's successes and lifted each other up during moments of doubt. Together, they were an unstoppable force, united by their shared vision of exploring the universe and creating innovative inventions for the world.

But the power of the mastermind went beyond just knowledge and ideas. It provided a support system that extended far beyond the walls of their meetings. When one member faced a setback, the others offered words of encouragement and shared their own experiences of overcoming challenges. They became a pillar of strength for each other.

As time passed, the mastermind alliance became more than just a group of individuals working towards a common goal. They became a family, bonded by their shared passion and their unwavering support for one another. Together, they navigated the ups and downs of their scientific pursuits, celebrating breakthroughs and conquering obstacles as a team.

Through the power of collaboration, Malachi and Malika realised that their dreams were not solitary endeavours. They discovered that by aligning themselves with like-minded individuals and forming a mastermind alliance, they could overcome any obstacle in their path. They learned to lean on each other's strengths and provide guidance when needed, creating a network of support that propelled them towards success.

With their newfound alliance, Malachi and Malika felt invincible. They were no longer alone in their pursuit of scientific knowledge and exploration. They had a dedicated group of friends who believed in them, challenged them, and cheered them on every step of the way.

Malachi and Malika reflected on the transformation they had undergone. They understood that the power of collaboration was not just about achieving individual success; it was about elevating everyone in the group. They had discovered the true essence of the mastermind alliance: that by working together, they could achieve far more than they ever could have imagined.

With their minds bustling with ideas and their hearts filled with gratitude, Malachi and Malika embraced their mastermind alliance and embarked on their journey with renewed vigour. They knew that no challenge was too great, no dream too ambitious when they had the power of collaboration by their side. The power of their collaborative spirit would guide them, propelling them towards greatness, and forever etching their names among the stars.

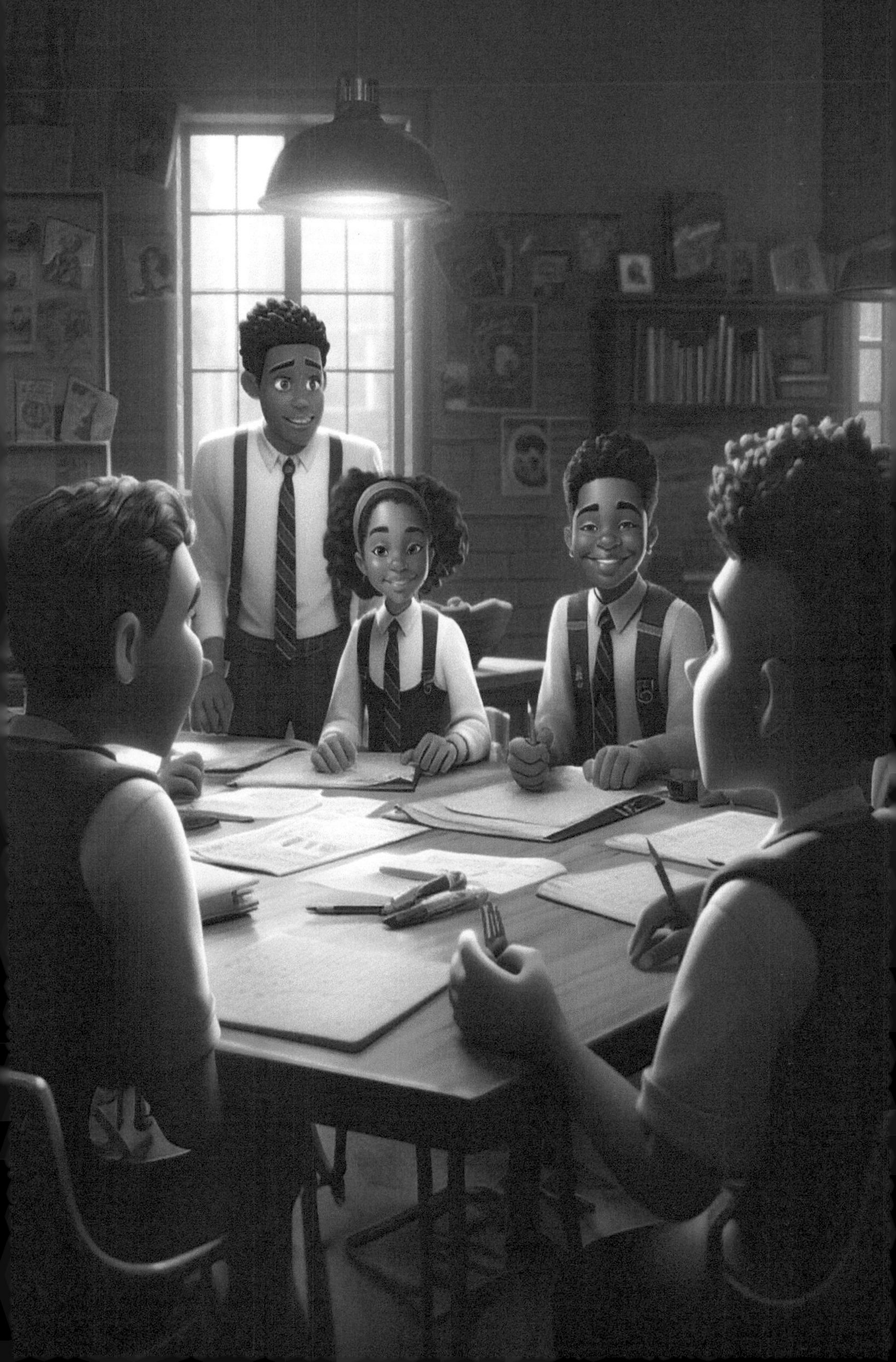

Activity: Mastermind Creation

- Form a Study Group: Gather a small group of friends who share a common interest or goal. It could be a subject you enjoy studying, a hobby you want to explore, or a project you want to work on together.

- Define the Purpose: Define the purpose of your study group. Is it to excel in a specific subject, learn a new skill, or complete a project? Clarifying the purpose will help you stay focused and aligned.

- Regular Meetings: Schedule regular meetings for your study group. It can be weekly, biweekly, or monthly, depending on everyone's availability. Consistency is key to building momentum and maintaining engagement.

- Share Knowledge and Resources: Share your knowledge and resources during the meetings. Each member can take turns presenting a topic, explaining a concept, or sharing interesting facts. This exchange of information will enhance everyone's understanding and broaden everyone's perspectives.

- Brainstorm and Discuss: Allocate time for brainstorming sessions and discussions. Ask questions, propose ideas, and engage in meaningful conversations related to your shared interest or goal. This will stimulate critical thinking, creativity, and collaboration.

- Support and Encouragement: It is important to provide support and encouragement to one another. Celebrate each other's achievements, offer constructive feedback, and provide assistance when needed. This positive and supportive environment will boost motivation and foster a sense of camaraderie.

- Set Individual Goals: Everyone sets individual goals related to their shared interest or goal. These goals can be specific, measurable, achievable, relevant, and time-bound (SMART). Each member can share their goals with the group, and the group can offer accountability and support to help them stay on track.

- Collaboration on Projects: Collaborate on projects that align with your shared interest. Work together on research, experiments, creative endeavours, or any other hands-on activities. This collaborative approach will foster teamwork, problem-solving, and project management skills.

- Seek External Expertise: Reach out to experts or mentors in your chosen field. You can invite guest speakers to your study group meetings or arrange virtual meetings with professionals who can provide insights and guidance. This will broaden your perspectives and expose you to real-world experiences.

- Reflect and Evaluate: At the end of each meeting or project, reflect on your progress and evaluate your experiences. Ask questions like: What did we learn? What worked well? What could we improve? This reflection will help you refine your approach and continuously improve your mastermind group dynamics.

By engaging in this activity, you will experience the power of the mastermind first-hand. You will learn the value of collaboration, collective intelligence, and shared support. The activity will foster a sense of belonging, enhance your learning experience, and encourage you to reach new heights in your chosen area of interest or goal.

Your Reflections

12

～

The Power Within: The Mystery of Energy Transmutation

As Malachi and Malika continued their journey of personal growth and discovery, the guardian introduced them to the concept of energy transmutation, Chapter 11 of 'Think and Grow Rich'. With eager anticipation, they gathered around the guardian, ready to unlock the secrets of this powerful principle.

The guardian observed their enthusiasm and began, "The tenth principle is the Mystery of Energy Transmutation. Everything in the universe is made up of energy. Energy is neither created nor destroyed but can be transformed and directed."

Malika's eyes widened with wonder. "How does energy transmutation help us in our pursuit of scientific exploration?" she asked, her voice filled with curiosity.

The guardian smiled. "Understanding that everything in the universe is made up of energy, including your thoughts and emotions, is essential," he explained. "By consciously harnessing and directing your energy, you can create positive change in your lives."

Malachi pondered the concept. "So, by transmuting our energy, harnessing and directing it, this will help us uncover new knowledge and make significant contributions to scientific exploration?"

The guardian nodded, captivated by Malachi's discernment. "Indeed, Malachi. As energy is neither created nor destroyed but transformed and directed, you can channel your energies into what you want to create rather than wasting it on negative things that don not serve you."

Malika definitely wanted to learn more on this concept, "How can we begin to transmute our energy? What steps can we take?"

The guardian's eyes gleamed. "To illustrate this concept, let me share an example with you?" he suggested.

He placed a bowl of water in front of Malachi and Malika and asked them to observe the stillness of the water. "Just like the water", the guardian explained "our energy can sometimes become stagnant and unproductive. But with conscious effort, we can transform it into something powerful and purposeful."

Malachi enquired about their next steps. "Are there any practices or techniques that can help us to transmute our energy?"

The guardian nodded, smiled and explained. "Practices such as meditation exercises. Connect with your inner energy and visualise it flowing through your bodies, cleansing away any negativity and replacing it with confidence and positivity," he advised.

"It's important to maintain a positive mindset and surround yourselves with uplifting influences. Read stories of great inventors, athletes, and artists who have harnessed the power of energy transmutation to achieve remarkable feats. Feel inspired by these stories and understood that you too have the ability to shape your own destinies."

Malika, feeling empowered, enthusiastically asked. "So, by transmuting our energy, we can expand our knowledge, make discoveries, and truly become scientists of the cosmos?"

The guardian smiled, his heart filled with pride. "Absolutely, Malika. Energy transmutation is a powerful tool to help you explore, discover, and make profound contributions to the scientific community. Embrace the unknown, and let your passion for the cosmos guide you on an extraordinary adventure."

As the chapter ended, Malachi and Malika reflected on the transformation they had experienced through energy transmutation. They understood that by consciously directing their energy and aligning it with their goals, they could create a life filled with abundance, success, and fulfilment.

~~~~~~

Malachi and Malika found themselves in a period of uncertainty. Though they had learned about the concept of energy transmutation, they struggled to apply it consistently in their lives. The journey towards mastering this powerful principle proved to be more challenging than they anticipated.

They encountered moments of self-doubt and frustration as they grappled with redirecting their energy towards positive thoughts and emotions. Negative thoughts seemed to creep in, creating a cloud of doubt around their dreams. They wondered if they were truly capable of harnessing the power within.

Feeling disheartened, Malachi and Malika reached out to the mentor for guidance. The mentor reassured them that their struggles were a natural part of the learning process. He explained that energy transmutation required consistent practice and dedication.

To help them overcome their challenges, the mentor suggested a series of exercises. He encouraged Malachi and Malika to keep a gratitude journal, where they could write down three things they were grateful for each day. This simple practice helped shift their focus towards positive aspects of their lives and gradually transformed their energy.

Additionally, the mentor reminded them of affirmations—positive statements they could repeat daily to reprogram their subconscious mind. Malachi and Malika had chosen affirmations that resonated with their goals and aspirations. They repeated them aloud with conviction, slowly replacing self-doubt with confidence.

However, even with these tools, Malachi and Malika still faced moments of setbacks. Old habits and negative thought patterns would resurface, testing their determination. It was during these trying times that they realised the true power of perseverance.

They reminded themselves that energy transmutation was not an instant solution, but a lifelong practice. They understood that setbacks were temporary and served as opportunities for growth. Instead of succumbing to negativity, they embraced these challenges as stepping stones towards their transformation.

Gradually, with unwavering persistence, Malachi and Malika noticed a shift within themselves. They became more aware of their thoughts and emotions, actively redirecting their energy towards positive channels. They celebrated even the smallest victories, knowing that each step forward brought them closer to mastering energy transmutation.

As they reflected on their journey, Malachi and Malika realised that struggles were an essential part of their growth. They discovered that true mastery of energy transmutation required patience, self-compassion, and a deep understanding of their own inner power.

Activity: The Power of Energy Transformation:

Energy Transforming Art

Materials needed:

Paper or canvas

- Assorted art supplies (crayons, coloured pencils, markers, paints, etc.)
- Magazines or printed images
- Glue or tape

Instructions:

- Energy can be transformed into different forms, just like how we can transform our emotions and thoughts into something positive and creative.
- Think of a specific emotion or energy you would like to transform. It could be sadness, anger, fear, or any other emotion you would like to shift towards a more positive state.
- Using art supplies, create a piece of artwork that represents the energy you wish to transform. You can use colours, shapes, and symbols to express your emotions visually.
- If available, use magazines or printed images that you can cut out and incorporate into your artwork to add more depth and meaning.
- Once you have completed your artwork, write a note about how you transformed your initial energy into something positive and creative. Explain the symbolism behind your artwork and how it represents your transformed energy.

• Display your artwork in a designated area to serve as a reminder of your ability to transform and redirect your energy towards positive and creative endeavours.

By engaging in this activity, you can learn to recognise and channel your emotions in a productive and creative way. It encourages self-expression, self-awareness, and the understanding that you have the power to transform your energy into something positive.

Your Reflections

13

∽

The Hidden Gems: Your Subconscious Superpowers

Malachi and Malika eagerly delved into Chapter 12 of 'Think and Grow Rich', eager to unravel the mysteries that lay hidden within their own minds. They we aware that the subconscious mind is a powerful tool that they can use to achieve their dreams of becoming inventors and scientists exploring the universe.

The guardian observed their elation and began, "Your subconscious mind is like a vast ocean, full of untapped potential and hidden treasures. It holds the key to unlocking your deepest desires and manifesting them into reality."

Intrigued, Malachi and Malika listened intently as the guardian explained, "Your conscious mind is like the captain of a ship, guiding your thoughts and actions. But it is your subconscious mind that serves as the engine, propelling you forward and influencing your beliefs, emotions, and habits."

Malika's eyes gleamed with marvel. "How does our subconscious mind help us on our journey to becoming inventors and scientists exploring the universe?" she asked eagerly.

The guardian smiled, acknowledging her curiosity. " The subconscious mind is like a powerful computer in our brains that works constantly in the background, processing information and influencing our thoughts and actions. It controls our beliefs, emotions, habits, and behaviours, and it has a big impact on our lives."

Malachi leaned forward, his mind racing with potentials. "So, by programming our subconscious mind, we can influence our thoughts to overcome challenges and keep moving forward on our path to scientific exploration?"

The guardian nodded, impressed by Malachi's understanding. "Indeed, Malachi. The subconscious mind is a powerful tool that you can use to achieve your goals. By programming it with positive thoughts and beliefs, and using visualisation techniques, you can tap into its power and unlock your full potential."

Malachi, once again, contemplated their next steps. "Are there any techniques or practices that can help us tap into the power of our subconscious mind?"

The guardian nodded, knowing he would ask. "The subconscious mind is like a fertile garden. Whatever seeds you plant within it, be they positive or negative, will grow and manifest in your life. By cultivating positive thoughts, beliefs, and emotions, you can create a harmonious environment for your dreams to flourish. Program your subconscious mind with positive affirmations and visualisations about your goals and desires. Repeat these affirmations to yourself every day, and over time, you will reprogram your subconscious mind to achieve your goals."

Malika asked excitedly. "So, hy embracing the power of our sub-conscious mind, we can unlock our potential and continue on our path towards scientific exploration of the universe?"

The guardian smiled, beaming with pride. "Absolutely, Malika. The key to unlocking your potential and achieving your dreams lay within your own subconscious mind."

Malachi and Malika closed the book, filled with the power of the subconscious mind. Through this experience, they learned that the sub-conscious mind is a powerful tool that they can use to achieve their goals. By programming it with positive thoughts and beliefs, and using visualisation techniques, they can tap into its power and unlock their full potential.

~~~~~~

Malachi and Malika found themselves facing a formidable challenge as they sought to harness the power of the subconscious mind. Despite their determination, they discovered that cultivating this power required patience, persistence, and a deep understanding of their own inner workings.

At first, the concept seemed straightforward enough. They under-stood that their thoughts, beliefs, and emotions played a crucial role in shaping their reality. They eagerly embraced affirmations and visualisa-tions, hoping for instant transformation and tangible results.

But as days turned into weeks and weeks into months, doubts began to creep into their minds. Despite their consistent efforts, they struggled to see the tangible changes they had hoped for. Negative thoughts and old patterns of self-doubt would occasionally resurface, threatening to undermine their progress.

Confused and disheartened, Malachi and Malika sought guidance from their wise mentor. They explained their frustrations and expressed their doubts, wondering if they were doing something wrong or if they simply lacked the necessary ability to tap into the power of their subconscious minds.

The mentor listened attentively, his compassionate gaze assuring them that their struggles were not unique. He reminded them that the subconscious mind is like a vast, complex puzzle—one that requires time, patience, and a willingness to explore its depths.

"You must remember," the mentor began, "that the subconscious mind operates on its own timeline. It may take longer than expected to reprogram old beliefs and patterns deeply ingrained within you. But rest assured, progress is being made, even if it is not immediately evident."

He encouraged Malachi and Malika to approach their journey with self-compassion and a gentle understanding of their own limitations. Instead of berating themselves for not seeing immediate results, they were to acknowledge their efforts and trust that the seeds they had planted were gradually taking root.

To help them navigate through this struggle, the mentor introduced new tools and practices. He guided them in incorporating meditation and mindfulness into their daily routines, teaching them to quiet their minds and become more attuned to the present moment.

He also stressed the importance of self-reflection and introspection. Malachi and Malika began journaling, recording their thoughts, feelings, and observations. Through this practice, they gained valuable insights into their subconscious patterns and discovered hidden beliefs that had been holding them back.

As the days turned into weeks and the weeks into months, Malachi and Malika noticed subtle shifts within themselves. They began to catch negative thoughts before they took hold, replacing them with positive affirmations and empowering beliefs. They recognised that progress was not always linear, but rather a series of small victories that accumulated over time.

The mentor reminded them that persistence was key. He shared stories of renowned individuals who had faced similar struggles on their own paths to success. They learned that setbacks and doubts were natural parts of the journey, and it was through perseverance and unwavering faith that breakthroughs were achieved.

Armed with this newfound understanding and renewed determination, Malachi and Malika recommitted themselves to their practice. They found solace in knowing that the power of the subconscious mind was not easily harnessed, but that every effort they made contributed to their growth and eventual success.

They embraced the struggle as an opportunity for self-discovery and personal development. They recognised that cultivating the power of the subconscious mind was not a destination, but rather an ongoing journey of self-mastery, not something to be conquered but rather embraced and cultivated over time.

With each passing day, their confidence grew. They could feel the subtle shifts within their minds and hearts, as limiting beliefs were replaced with empowering ones. They became more attuned to their intuition, trusting its guidance as they navigated their paths.

Malachi and Malika learned that the struggle itself was an integral part of their transformation. Through it, they developed resilience, patience, and an unwavering commitment to their goals.

As their journey continued, they knew that their struggles would ebb and flow. But armed with newfound wisdom and the support of their mentor, Malachi and Malika were ready to face any challenges that came their way. They had learned that the power of the subconscious mind was a journey of self-discovery, a constant invitation to explore the depths of their own potential.

And so, with hope in their spirits and an unwavering belief in the power of their subconscious minds, Malachi and Malika pressed on, eager to uncover the limitless possibilities that awaited them.

Activity: Activate the Subconscious Mind

Dream Collage

Materials needed:

- Poster board or a large sheet of paper
- Scissors
- Glue or tape
- Magazines or printed images
- Markers or coloured pencils

Instructions:

Our subconscious mind is like a powerful library of thoughts, memories, and dreams that can help us achieve our goals and aspirations.

- Think about your dreams and goals. Imagine your ideal future and what you want to accomplish.
- Use magazines or printed images cut out images and words that represent your dreams and goals. You can look for pictures of places you want to visit, activities you want to do, or careers you want to pursue.
- Using a poster board or a large sheet of paper, arrange and glue the images and words you've cut out onto the board, creating a collage that represents your dreams and goals.
- Once the collages are complete, write a note about the images and words you chose. Explain why each item is important to you and how it relates to your dreams and goals.
- Display your dream collages in a prominent place, such as your

bedroom wall. This will serve as a visual reminder of your aspirations and help program your subconscious mind to work towards those goals.

Your subconscious mind is always at work, even when you're not consciously thinking about your dreams and goals. Trust in your inner power and believe in your ability to achieve what you desire.

By engaging in this activity, you can visually express your dreams and goals, helping to embed them in your subconscious mind. The collage serves as a powerful reminder of your aspirations and encourages your subconscious mind to work towards those goals even when you're not consciously thinking about them. It's a creative and fun way for you to tap into the power of your subconscious mind and start manifesting your dreams into reality.

Your Reflections

14

~∾~

Brain Blast: Your Mind's Limitless Potential

Malachi and Malika eagerly turned the pages of 'Think and Grow Rich' to unveil the twelfth principle: The Brain. They knew that to become inventors and scientists exploring the universe, they needed to understand how the brain works.

The guardian, noticing their enthusiasm, began, "Your brain is like a powerful tool that you can use to achieve your dreams and goals. It has the ability to create new ideas and solve problems. But to do that, you have to train your brain to think in a certain way."

Malachi inclined forward, eager to grasp the concept. "How can the brain help us to become inventors and scientists exploring the universe?" he asked.

The guardian grinned, appreciating Malachi's interest. "Well, Malachi, we've actually been doing that for a while now, that is, by feeding it positive thoughts and ideas. When you think positively, your brain releases chemicals that make you feel good, which in turn motivates you to act and achieve your goals. Therefore, it's important to always think positively and surround yourself with positive people,"

Malika nodded, her eyes gleaming. "So, it's important to train you brain with positive affirmations, visualisations and goal setting to achieve our dreams?"

The guardian nodded in agreement. "Absolutely, Malika. Setting goals for yourself and working towards achieving them helps to create new neural pathways in your brain, which can help you become more focused and determined. Your brain is a powerful tool, and you can use it to achieve anything you set your mind to."

Malachi stroked his chin, contemplating their next steps. " What else can we do to train our brain?"

The guardian turned and smiled. "Excellent question, Malachi. The brain is like a supercomputer, capable of processing vast amounts of information, making connections, and solving complex problems. By harnessing the power of your brain, you can propel yourself closer to your dream of becoming inventors and scientists exploring the universe. Focus on maintaining a positive mindset. Your thoughts and beliefs have a direct impact on your brain's performance. So, cultivate a mindset of optimism and resilience. Replace self-doubt with self-belief and turn setbacks into learning opportunities. By nurturing a positive mindset, you can unleash the full power of your brain."

Malachi and Malika exchanged determined glances, knowing that they were going to learn about the incredible capabilities of the human brain which is key to unlocking their potential as scientists exploring the universe.

The guardian concluded, "Remember, my young seekers, your brain is your most powerful tool. Continuously nourishing, challenging, and believing in your amazing brain, you can overcome any obstacle and reach for the stars."

Malachi and Malika closed the book, their minds racing with the probabilities that lay ahead. They understood that by harnessing the power of their brain, they would become unstoppable in their pursuit of exploring the universe.

~~~~~~

Malachi and Malika were now well-versed in the principles of Think and Grow Rich, but their journey was far from over. Their mentor, knowing the immense power of the human brain, decided it was time to delve into the twelfth principle: The Brain.

As they gathered around a table filled with books and diagrams, the mentor began to explain the wonders of the brain. He spoke about its complexity, it's incredible capacity for learning and adaptation, and how it controlled every aspect of their thoughts, emotions, and actions.

Malachi and Malika listened intently, their curiosity piqued. They realised that understanding the brain was key to unlocking their true potential and achieving their dreams.

The mentor guided them through fascinating experiments and inter-active activities designed to explore the different regions of the brain. They discovered the importance of neural pathways and how their thoughts and experiences shaped the connections within their brains.

They learned that the brain was like a muscle, and just like any muscle, it could be trained and strengthened. The mentor encouraged them to engage in activities that challenged their minds, such as puzzles, creative projects, and learning new skills.

Through these exercises, Malachi and Malika witnessed the incredible plasticity of the brain. They saw how, with consistent effort and practice, they could rewire their brains to think more positively, overcome obstacles, and achieve their goals.

The mentor shared inspiring stories of individuals who had achieved great success by harnessing the power of their brains. They learned about inventors, scientists, and artists who had tapped into their creativity and used their brains to envision ground-breaking ideas and innovations.

To further deepen their understanding, the mentor introduced them to the concept of neuroplasticity. They discovered that their brains were constantly changing and adapting, even in adulthood. This realisation filled them with a sense of optimism and excitement for the endless possibilities that lay ahead.

Malachi and Malika began to appreciate the significance of their thoughts and beliefs. They understood that their brain's response to external stimuli was influenced by their mindset. They learned to cultivate positive thoughts, reframe negative experiences, and embrace a growth mindset that empowered them to overcome challenges.

In one particularly memorable experiment, they explored the concept of visualisation again. The mentor guided them through a meditation where they imagined themselves achieving their wildest dreams. They visualised every detail, allowing their brains to create neural connections that strengthened their belief in their own abilities.

Throughout their journey, Malachi and Malika discovered the importance of taking care of their brains. They learned about the significance of sleep, nutrition, and exercise in maintaining optimal brain health. They committed to nurturing their minds and bodies to ensure they could operate at their highest potential.

Malachi and Malika felt a profound sense of gratitude for the incredible gift they possessed—their brains. They understood that with the right mindset and consistent effort, they could tap into its immense power and achieve extraordinary things.

Armed with this newfound knowledge, they eagerly embraced the principle of The Brain, knowing that it held the key to unlocking their limitless potential. They felt a renewed sense of purpose and determination to continue their journey, fuelled by the boundless capabilities of their minds.

And so, with a deep appreciation for the intricacies of their brains and a sense of awe for the wonders that lay within, Malachi and Malika ventured forward, ready to embrace every opportunity and challenge that came their way.

Little did they know that their understanding of The Brain would be the catalyst for their greatest adventures yet.

Activity: The Brain

Brain Teasers and Puzzles

Materials needed:

- Brain teaser books or printed brain teasers and puzzles
- Paper and pencils

Instructions:

Brain teasers and puzzles are fun challenges that require thinking, problem-solving, and creativity.

- Get some brain teaser books or print out a variety of brain teasers and puzzles. Ensure that the difficulty level matches your age group.
- Read the instructions for each brain teaser or puzzle and work individually or in a small group (study group / mastermind group) to solve them.
- Give yourself ample time to think and come up with your solutions. Use your brains creatively and critically to find the answers.
- Keep a record of the brain teasers you have solved and challenge yourself to find new brain teasers.
- Notice the importance of persistence, creativity, and problem-solving skills in tackling brain teasers. These skills are part of harnessing the power of your amazing brain.
- Challenge yourself and create your own brain teasers or puzzles and share them with your peers.

By engaging in brain teasers and puzzles, you can exercise your brain muscles, enhance your problem-solving skills, and explore different approaches to challenges. This activity encourages you to think critically, tap into your creativity, and appreciate the incredible power of your own brains. It's a fun and engaging way for you to implement and celebrate the wonders of your amazing brains.

15

~

Sense of Wonder: Awaken Your Extraordinary Abilities

Anticipation filled the air as Malachi and Malika turned to the next chapter in 'Think and Grow Rich', eager to explore the six sense. The last few steps were challenging to comprehend; however, they did grasp the concept. They realised that so far, the principles seemed to intertwine with each other, as you practice one step, you naturally embodied some of the other steps as they all come together as one.

The guardian noticed their excitement and smiled warmly. "The sixth sense is a power of intuition that we all possess, but most of us don't use it. It's like having a hidden sense that allows us to know things without any logical explanation. It is a unique and mysterious concept that has been studied and explored by great thinkers throughout history. It is often described as a "gut feeling" or intuition that helps guide people towards their goals and dreams."

Malachi and Malika were even more curious now. They wanted to know how they could use their sixth sense to become successful in life.

"How does the six sense help us become inventors and scientists exploring the universe?" Malika asked.

The guardian nodded, understanding her quest for knowledge. "To develop your sixth sense, you need to learn to listen to your inner voice, your gut feeling. It is the voice that guides you when you are in doubt or facing a difficult decision."

Malachi leaned forward, his mind buzzing with ideas. "So, we need to listen to our gut feelings, that feeling that tells us to do or not do something sometimes?"

The guardian nodded, impressed by Malachi's insight. "Absolutely, Malachi. That inner voice is your intuition, your sixth sense. It can guide you to make the right decisions in life, and it is always available to you. You just need to learn to listen to it."

Malika couldn't contain her excitement. "But how do we harness the power of our intuition? How do we strengthen it?"

The guardian smiled, sensing their eagerness to learn. " You can start by paying attention to your dreams. Dreams can be a way for the subconscious mind to communicate with the conscious mind, and they can reveal valuable insights. Keep a dream journal, write down your dreams every morning. Notice that your dreams often provide you with answers to your problems or questions you have been thinking about."

Malachi furrowed his brow, contemplating their next steps. "So, by cultivating our six sense, and listening to and trusting our intuition, we can make better decisions and navigate the complexities of our scientific pursuits?

The guardian nodded, impressed by Malachi's grasp of the concept. "Exactly, Malachi. In moments of doubt or uncertainty, turn to your sixth sense for guidance. Quiet your mind, tune into your intuition, and ask for clarity. The answers will come to you in various forms, in inspired thoughts, intuitive hunches, or coincidences that align with your goals."

Malika couldn't help but ask, "Is there anything else we can do to strengthen our intuition?"

The guardian nodded approvingly. " To develop your sixth sense further, Embraced silence and solitude. Meditate. In moments of quiet reflection, your intuition becomes clearer and more pronounced. Practiced meditation and mindfulness, allowing your mind to quiet down and connect with the deeper wisdom within. In these moments of stillness, you will find answers to questions you haven't even asked yet."

Malachi and Malika exchanged excited glances, realising that their intuition held the key to internal wisdom and guidance.

The guardian concluded, "Remember, my young seekers, learn to trust these messages from your sixth sense and act upon them with confidence. Understood that by tapping into your sixth sense, you are tapping into the infinite wisdom of the universe itself."

Malachi and Malika closed the book, their minds buzzing with the endless potential their intuition held. They knew that by embracing the power of their intuition, they were one step closer to realising their dreams of becoming inventors and scientists exploring the universe.

~~~~~~

Malachi and Malika had come a long way on their journey to uncover the secrets of Think and Grow Rich. They had delved into the power of the mind, harnessed their imagination, and tapped into the wisdom of their subconscious. Now, they faced a new challenge – cultivating their intuition.

Their mentor, recognising the importance of intuition in decision-making and goal attainment, guided them through a series of exercises designed to develop this innate ability. They gathered in a tranquil garden, surrounded by vibrant flowers and whispering trees, ready to embark on this enlightening endeavour.

The mentor explained that intuition was the voice within, the guiding light that could help them navigate through uncertainty and make choices aligned with their deepest desires. It was a subtle but powerful force that would lead them towards their goals if they learned to listen and trust it.

Malachi and Malika understood the significance of this lesson, yet they found it challenging to tune in to their intuition. Doubts and distractions often clouded their minds, making it difficult to hear the gentle whispers of their inner wisdom. They longed to develop a stronger connection to their intuition, knowing that it held the key to unlocking their path to success.

With the mentor's guidance, they embarked on a journey of self-reflection and self-awareness. They learned to quiet their minds through meditation and mindfulness practices, allowing the noise of the world to fade away and create space for their intuition to emerge.

In nature, they found solace and inspiration. They took long walks, observing the beauty of the world around them and reconnecting with the rhythms of the earth. They learned to listen to the whispers of the wind, the rustling of leaves, and the melody of birds, recognising that nature held wisdom that could guide them.

The mentor encouraged them to journal their thoughts and feelings, providing a safe space for self-expression and introspection. Through writing, they discovered patterns and insights that revealed the guidance of their intuition. They learned to trust their gut feelings and inner nudges, even when they couldn't fully explain or rationalise them.

As they continued their journey, Malachi and Malika realised that cultivating intuition required stillness, patience, and trust. They learned to differentiate between the voice of fear and doubt and the soft, reassuring voice of their intuition. They discovered that their intuition often spoke to them through symbols, dreams, and synchronicities, offering gentle nudges and signs to guide them on their path.

The mentor shared stories of great inventors, scientists, and visionaries who had relied on their intuition to make ground-breaking discoveries and create revolutionary inventions. Malachi and Malika felt inspired and encouraged, knowing that they were tapping into a power that had shaped the world throughout history.

In one particularly powerful exercise, the mentor led them through a guided visualisation. They closed their eyes, allowed their minds to wander, and envisioned themselves living their dreams. They felt the joy, excitement, and fulfilment as if it were happening in that very moment. Through this practice, they connected with their intuition on a deeper level, allowing it to guide them towards their true desires.

As their journey progressed, Malachi and Malika began to recognise the signs and synchronicities that appeared in their lives. They learned to trust their intuition as a reliable compass, guiding them to make decisions aligned with their authentic selves and their goals.

With each step forward, they grew more confident in their ability to cultivate their intuition. They embraced the uncertainty of the journey, knowing that their intuition would light the way. They let go of the need for instant answers and trusted that the answers would reveal themselves at the right time.

Malachi and Malika felt a newfound sense of empowerment. They knew that cultivating their intuition was an ongoing practice, one that required dedication and trust. But they also realised that their intuition was a valuable gift, a guiding force that would lead them towards their dreams.

With their intuition as their faithful companion, Malachi and Malika were ready to take the next step towards their goals, knowing that they possessed an inner wisdom that would never steer them wrong.

Activity: Activate your Sixth Sense

Intuition Exercises

Materials needed:

• Paper and pencils

Instructions:

Intuition is a powerful tool that can guide you towards making the right decisions and finding answers to your questions.

Intuition can manifest in different ways, such as gut feelings, hunches, or sudden insights.

• Sit quietly and focus on your breathing. Clear your minds and create a calm and relaxed state.
• After a few moments, think of a question or a situation you need guidance or insight on. It could be something as simple as choosing what book to read or deciding on an activity for the day.
• Write down your question or situation on a piece of paper.
• Close your eyes and visualise the question or situation in your mind. Imagine different scenarios and possibilities.
• Pay attention to any thoughts, feelings, or images that come to your mind. These could be subtle impressions or flashes of insight.
• After a few minutes, open your eyes and write down any intuitive thoughts or insights you received during the exercise.
• Reflect on your intuitive insights and how you felt when receiving them.

- Trust your intuition and use it as a guide in your everyday life. Listen to your inner voice and act upon the insights you receive.
- Repeat this activity periodically, explore and develop your intuitive abilities further. Practice with different questions or situations to strengthen your connection to your sixth sense.

By engaging in intuition exercises, you can tap into your inner wisdom and develop your sixth sense. Trust your instincts, listen to your inner voice, and make decisions based on your intuitive insights. You possess a powerful tool within yourself, which can guide you towards making wise choices and finding solutions to your problems.

Remember, intuition is like a muscle that gets stronger with practice.

Your Reflections

16

～

Stay Strong: Outwit the Six Ghosts of Fear

Malachi and Malika had come a long way on their journey towards achieving their goals. They had faced numerous challenges, but their determination and the principles they had learned from Think and Grow Rich had guided them thus far. However, there was one final obstacle they needed to overcome—the six ghosts of fear.

The guardian gathered Malachi and Malika around him, ready to explain the concept of the six ghosts of fear. He wanted to give them a clear understanding of what they were up against so that they could conquer their fears and move forward with confidence.

"Dreams and goals are wonderful things, but sometimes we can be held back by fear. There are six ghosts of fear that often haunt us and try to keep us from reaching our full potential.

The first ghost is the fear of poverty. It's the worry that we won't have enough money or resources to pursue our dreams. But remember, by acquiring knowledge and skills, we can create opportunities and overcome this fear.

The second ghost is the fear of criticism. It's the fear of what others might think or say about our dreams. But always remember to believe in yourselves and surround yourselves with supportive people who encourage and uplift you.

The third ghost is the fear of ill health. It's the worry that we won't have the physical or mental strength to chase our dreams. Take care of your bodies and minds through exercise, healthy eating, and self-care. This will give you the energy you need to pursue your goals.

The fourth ghost is the fear of loss of love. It's the fear of disappointing or losing the love and support of those around us. While it's important to have support, never forget to love and believe in yourselves. Your self-worth is essential.

The fifth ghost is the fear of old age. It's the concern that time is running out and we won't have enough time to achieve our dreams. Stay focused on your goals, manage your time wisely, and remember that it's never too late to pursue what you desire.

The sixth ghost is the fear of death. It's the fear of the unknown and the thought that we won't leave a lasting impact. Embrace each day, live with purpose, and make a positive difference in the world. That way, your legacy will endure.

"Remember, my dear children, these fears are natural, but they shouldn't control us. With courage, determination, and the principles of Think and Grow Rich, we can outwit these ghosts of fear and achieve greatness. Trust in yourselves and believe that you have the power to overcome any fear that stands in your way." The guardian explained.

Malachi and Malika listened intently, absorbing the wisdom the guardian shared. They felt empowered, knowing that they had the tools to conquer their fears and pursue their dreams. With newfound confidence, they eagerly embarked on their journey, ready to face the ghosts of fear head-on and emerge victorious.

~~~~~~

Malachi and Malika stood at the precipice of their dreams, their hearts pounding with both excitement and trepidation. They had come so far on their journey, but now they faced their ultimate challenge—the battle against their deepest fears and doubts.

As they gazed into the mirror of self-reflection, their fears stared back at them, threatening to hold them back from reaching their full potential. Doubts crept into their minds, whispering that they were not capable or worthy of achieving their goals. But they were determined to confront these fears head-on, armed with the knowledge they had gained and the unwavering support of their mentor.

Together, they embarked on a series of transformative exercises designed to dismantle the stronghold of fear. They engaged in deep introspection, uncovering the root causes of their fears and identifying the limiting beliefs that held them back. Through journaling, meditation, and open discussions, they peeled back the layers of doubt, exposing their vulnerabilities in the pursuit of growth.

The mentor shared stories of his own battles with fear and reassured Malachi and Malika that fear was a natural part of the journey towards success. They learned that even the most accomplished individuals had faced their own fears and doubts, but what set them apart was their ability to rise above them.

With newfound courage, Malachi and Malika confronted their fears one by one. They took small steps, pushing themselves beyond their comfort zones and proving to themselves that they were capable of more than they had ever imagined. Each victory, no matter how small, fuelled their determination and built a resilient mindset.

They also discovered the power of positive affirmations and visualisation. They began to replace their fearful thoughts with empowering beliefs, rewiring their minds for success. They imagined themselves overcoming challenges, achieving their goals, and embracing the transformation that awaited them on the other side of fear.

The journey was not without its setbacks. There were moments when self-doubt threatened to engulf them, but they turned to their mentor and each other for support. They reminded themselves of the progress they had made and the inner strength they had discovered along the way. With each setback, they grew more determined to forge ahead, refusing to let fear dictate their path.

As the final showdown approached, Malachi and Malika found themselves standing tall, their fear transformed into a fierce determination. They faced their deepest fears with unwavering resolve, armed with the knowledge that they had gained, the support of their mentor, and the belief in themselves.

In a climactic moment of triumph, they emerged on the other side, their fears vanquished and their spirits lifted. They had conquered the demons that once held them back, embracing the transformation that had taken place within their hearts and minds.

With newfound confidence, Malachi and Malika realised that they were unstoppable. They had discovered the secret to conquering fear and embracing transformation—the unwavering belief in their own abilities and the courage to face their fears head-on. They knew that they were destined for greatness and that their dreams were within reach.

As they stood hand in hand, ready to embark on the next phase of their journey, a sense of triumph washed over them. They had not only conquered their fears but had also unlocked a power within themselves that would continue to propel them forward.

With their hearts full of gratitude, for the lessons learned and the transformation experienced, Malachi and Malika knew that this chapter marked a new beginning—a chapter where they would continue to embrace growth, conquer challenges, and achieve greatness.

And so, with their fears left behind and their hearts ablaze with determination, Malachi and Malika stepped boldly into their bright and promising future.

Activity: Conquering the Six Ghosts of Fear

Materials needed:

- Paper, coloured pencils or markers

Instructions:

Consider the concept of the six ghosts of fear: fear of poverty, fear of criticism, fear of ill health, fear of loss of love, fear of old age, and fear of death.

These fears can sometimes hold us back from pursuing our dreams and achieving our goals.

- Get a piece of paper and divide it into six sections, labelling each section with one of the fears: poverty, criticism, ill health, loss of love, old age, and death.
- In each section, draw a picture or write a few words that represent a positive mindset or action you can take to overcome that particular fear.

For example:

- Fear of poverty: Draw a picture of a piggy bank and write "Learn about money and how to save and invest."
- Fear of criticism: Draw a shield and write "Believe in myself and surround myself with supportive people."

- Fear of ill health: Draw a person exercising and write "Take care of my body through healthy habits and exercise."
- Fear of loss of love: Draw a heart and write "Love myself and focus on my own dreams and goals."
- Fear of old age: Draw a clock and write "Make the most of every day and keep learning and growing."
- Fear of death: Draw a butterfly and write "Leave a positive impact and live a meaningful life."

- Reflect on how these strategies can be applied in your life. Remember these positive mindset approaches whenever you encounter fear or doubts about pursuing your dreams.

- Display your artwork in your room as a reminder of your ability to outwit the ghosts of fear and move forward with confidence.

By engaging in this activity, you can begin to develop a proactive mindset when faced with fear. You learn to identify positive strategies to overcome each fear and gain a sense of empowerment and resilience in pursuing your dreams and goals.

17

~

Dream Big, Shine Bright: Mastering the Art of Success

Malachi and Malika sat together, reflecting on their incredible journey of discovery and growth. They had explored the principles of 'Think and Grow Rich' and had unlocked the secrets to achieving their dreams of becoming inventors and scientists exploring the universe. Now, they were ready to explore the final principle - the essence of thinking and growing rich.

The guardian entered the room, wearing a warm smile. "Welcome to the final chapter," he said. "The essence of thinking and growing rich lies in understanding that true wealth goes beyond material possessions. It encompasses a rich and abundant life in all aspects - wealth of mind, body, and spirit."

Malachi looked thoughtful. "So, it's not just about acquiring money or possessions?" he asked.

The guardian nodded. "Exactly, Malachi. While financial abundance is one aspect, true wealth comes from nurturing your passions, relationships, health, and personal growth. It is about finding fulfilment and living a purpose-driven life."

Malika's eyes lit up. "But how do we cultivate this abundance in all areas of our lives?" she wondered.

The guardian paused for a moment, then replied, "It begins with your thoughts. Your thoughts shape your beliefs, actions, and ultimately, your reality. By cultivating a positive and abundance-focused mindset, you can attract opportunities, build meaningful relationships, and manifest your dreams."

Malachi leaned forward, eager to learn more. "Are there any specific practices or techniques that can help us develop this abundance mindset?"

The guardian smiled, pleased with Malachi's enthusiasm. "Yes, indeed. Practices such as gratitude, visualisation, and affirmations can help you align your thoughts and beliefs with the abundance you seek," he explained. "Practice gratitude daily, acknowledging the blessings in your life. Visualise your dreams and goals as if they have already come to fruition. Repeat positive affirmations that affirm your worthiness of abundance."

Malika contemplated the guardian's words. "So, by nurturing an abundance mindset, we can create a life filled with rich experiences, meaningful connections, and personal growth?" she responded.

The guardian nodded, his eyes filled with wisdom. "Exactly, Malika. When you align your thoughts, beliefs, and actions with abundance, you become a magnet for success and fulfilment. You attract the people, resources, and opportunities that support your growth and bring your dreams to life."

Malachi and Malika sat in quiet reflection, embracing the power of the final principle. They understood that true wealth encompassed much more than material possessions. It was about living a life of purpose, passion, and abundance in all areas.

As they closed the book on their incredible journey, they felt a profound sense of gratitude for the wisdom they had gained. They were now equipped with the knowledge and principles to think and grow rich, not only in their pursuit of scientific exploration and invention but in every aspect of their lives.

Their journey had just begun, and they were excited to apply the principles they had learned to create a life filled with abundance, success, and joy.

And so, with their hearts full of gratitude and minds filled with possibility, Malachi and Malika embarked on their lifelong journey of thinking and growing rich.

~~~~~~

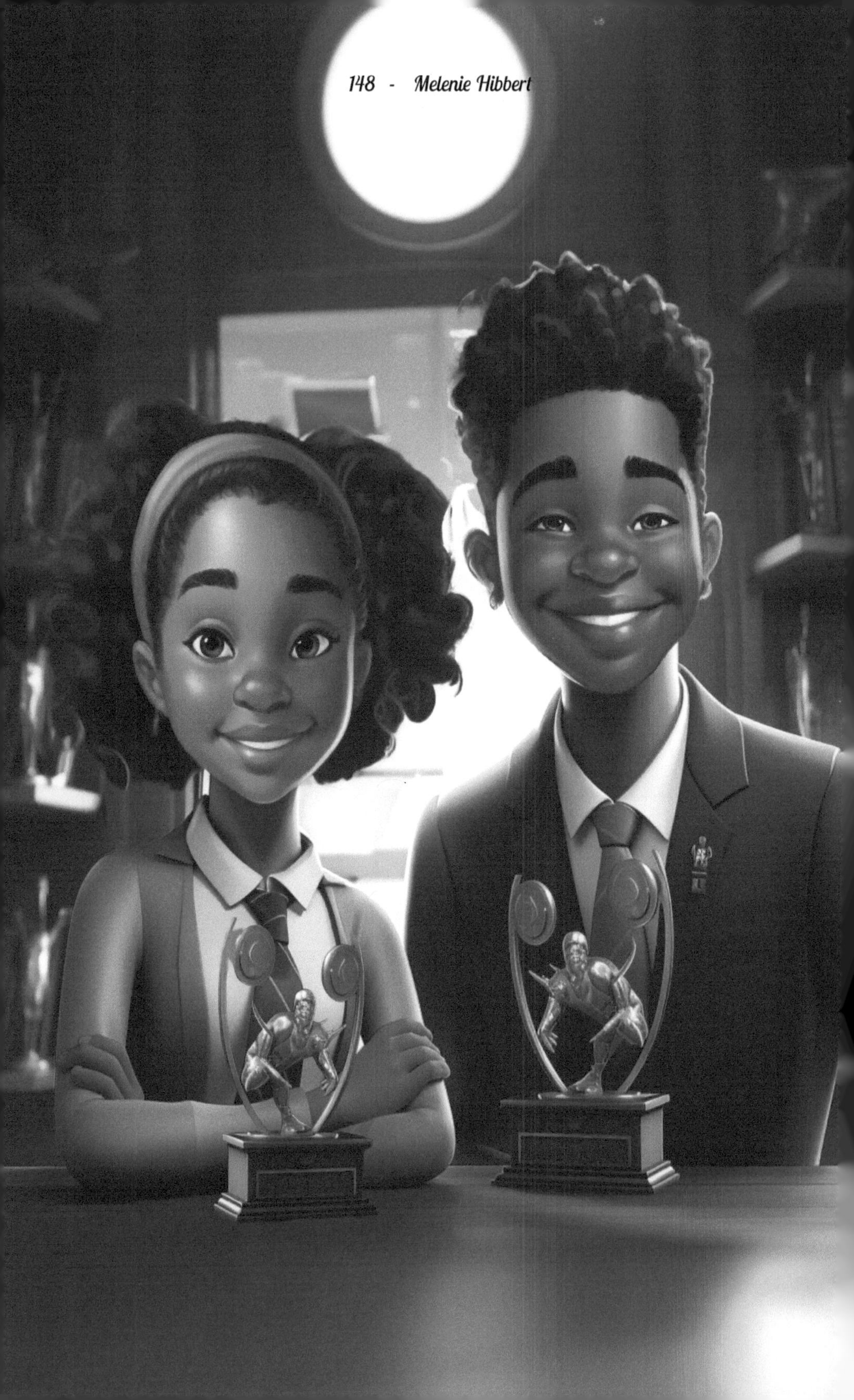

Epilogue: A New Beginning...

Malachi and Malika returned from their extraordinary journey, their hearts filled with a newfound sense of purpose and determination. The secrets of Think and Grow Rich had ignited a flame within them—a flame that would guide them towards their dreams and aspirations.

As they stepped back into their familiar surroundings, they couldn't help but notice how everything seemed different. The world appeared brighter, brimming with possibilities and opportunities. They had developed a keen awareness of their own potential and realised that they held the power to shape their destiny.

Armed with the principles they had learned, Malachi and Malika set forth on their individual paths, ready to conquer any challenge that came their way. They embraced the first principle, Desire, and allowed their dreams to fuel their actions. Their desires had become crystal clear, and they committed themselves wholeheartedly to their pursuit.

With unwavering faith in themselves and their dreams, Malachi and Malika stepped into the second principle: Faith. They knew that setbacks and obstacles might come their way, but their belief in their own abilities and the support of the universe propelled them forward. They faced each challenge with the unwavering conviction that they were capable of overcoming anything.

The third principle, Auto-Suggestion, became a daily practice for Malachi and Malika. They replaced negative thoughts with positive affirmations, rewiring their subconscious minds to support their dreams.

Through consistent self-talk and positive reinforcement, they built a strong foundation of belief in themselves and their abilities.

The fourth principle, Specialised Knowledge, became their compass as they delved deeper into their chosen fields. They sought out mentors, attended workshops and courses, and immersed themselves in the knowledge necessary to excel. They understood that expertise would set them apart and provide them with a competitive edge.

The power of their imagination, the fifth principle, became their secret weapon. They visualised their goals, creating vivid mental images of the future they desired. With each visualisation, their dreams felt more tangible, and they harnessed the power of their minds to bring them into reality.

In the sixth principle, Organised Planning, Malachi and Malika recognised the importance of setting clear goals and creating action plans. They broke down their dreams into manageable steps, mapping out the road ahead. They embraced structure and discipline, knowing that it would lead them closer to their desired destination.

The power of decision, the seventh principle, became their compass in times of uncertainty. They understood that indecision led to stagnation, so they made choices with conviction and confidence. They became adept at evaluating options, weighing risks, and committing wholeheartedly to their chosen paths.

With unwavering persistence, the eighth principle, Malachi and Malika pressed forward despite challenges and setbacks. They knew that success was not an overnight achievement but the result of consistent effort and determination. They kept their eyes fixed on the prize, refusing to be deterred by temporary obstacles.

The ninth principle, the Power of the Mastermind, guided their journey. They surrounded themselves with like-minded individuals who uplifted and supported them. Together, they formed a collective force, sharing ideas, insights, and encouragement. They celebrated each other's victories and provided a network of support through the inevitable ups and downs.

In their exploration of energy transmutation, the tenth principle became their guide. They marvelled at the power of channelling their energy into actions that moved them forward in pursuit of their goals. They expanded their horizons through focused energy, constantly seeking to learn and grow, knowing that the pursuit of knowledge was a lifelong journey.

They programmed their The Subconscious Mind, the eleventh principle, their super computer to influence their thoughts, behaviours and actions to continually work for them in progressing towards their goals.

They trained their amazing brain, the twelfth principle, to think in a certain way, to create new ideas and solve problems; to be the powerful tool that they can use to achieve their dreams and goals.

They used the power of their intuition – the six sense, the thirteenth principle to guide them on their path of discovery. They harnessed their natural ability to perceive things beyond the ordinary senses—an uncanny intuition that guides them towards the right path.

Finally, Malachi and Malika faced the six ghosts of fear, gaining a clear understanding of what they were up against and how they could conquer their fears and move forward with confidence.

Now, standing at the cusp of a new beginning, Malachi and Malika felt an indescribable sense of gratitude and excitement. They knew that they were equipped with the tools and principles to create a life of abundance and fulfilment. They were ready to embrace the challenges, knowing that they held within them the power to transform their lives and make a positive impact on the world.

As they set forth on their individual paths, their hearts intertwined with gratitude for the incredible journey they had experienced. They carried with them the wisdom of the ages and the understanding that their dreams were within reach.

And so, Malachi and Malika embarked on their new beginning, their spirits alight with the knowledge that they held the keys to unlock their limitless potential. With each step forward, they left a trail of inspiration for others to follow, sowing the seeds of success - a testament to the transformative power of Think and Grow Rich...

Your Reflections

As we come to the end of this book, I hope that you have learned a lot about the principles of Think and Grow Rich. These principles are not just for adults who want to be successful in business, but they are also for young people, like you, who have dreams and aspirations. These principles are the seeds of success for everything, every aspect of your life. You have the potential to be great and achieve anything you set your mind to.

Remember that success is not just about money or material possessions, but it is also about happiness and fulfilment. The principles of Think and Grow Rich can help you achieve success in all areas of your life.

I encourage you to continue learning and growing, and to always believe in yourself and your abilities. You have the power to create the life you want, so never give up on your dreams. Use the principles of My Genius Me as a guide and a roadmap to help you along the way.

As you grow older, you will face many challenges and obstacles in life. Some of these challenges may seem insurmountable, but if you remember the principles of My Genius Me, you can overcome them.

Remember to always have a positive attitude, to set clear goals for yourself, to take action towards those goals, and to never give up. Use your imagination and your creativity to come up with innovative solutions to problems, and use the power of your subconscious mind to help you achieve your goals.

And always remember that success is not just about what you accomplish, but it's also about the person you become along the way. It's about the values and the principles that guide you, and the impact that you have on the world around you.

So, continue to learn and grow, surround yourself with positive people who encourage and support you, and always believe in yourself. With these principles in mind, you can achieve anything you set your mind to and become the best version of yourself.

Finally, I want to leave you with this quote from Napoleon Hill, the author of Think and Grow Rich:

"Whatever the mind can conceive and believe, it can achieve."

Believe in yourself, and go out there and achieve your dreams!

Melenie Hibbert

Milton Keynes UK
Ingram Content Group UK Ltd.
UKHW051821181123
432797UK00001B/2